9/10

AT ITS
CENTERS

TEXAS PAN AMERICAN LITERATURE
IN TRANSLATION SERIES

Danny J. Anderson, Editor

AND LET THE EARTH TREMBLE AT ITS CENTERS

Gonzalo Celorio

———

TRANSLATED BY Dick Gerdes
FOREWORD BY Rubén Gallo

UNIVERSITY OF TEXAS PRESS ⬥ AUSTIN

TRANSLATION FUNDED BY THE
USA-MEXICO FUND FOR CULTURE,
2001–2002

LIBRARY OF CONGRESS CATALOGING-IN-PUBLICATION DATA

Celorio, Gonzalo.
    [Y retiemble en sus centros la tierra. English]
    And let the earth tremble at its centers / Gonzalo Celorio ;
translated by Dick Gerdes ; foreword by Rubén Gallo. — 1st ed.
    p.   cm. — (Texas Pan American literature in translation series)
    ISBN 978-0-292-71911-8 (cloth : alk. paper) —
    ISBN 978-0-292-71962-0 (pbk. : alk. paper)
    I. Gerdes, Dick.   II. Title.
    PQ7298.13.E56Y613   2009
    863'.64—dc22

                                         2008034264

FOR HERNÁN LARA ZAVALA

———

I was thirsty and you gave me drink.

—MATTHEW 25:35

Above all, it's necessary to be thirsty.

—CATHERINE OF SIENA

*My thirst for love will be like an iron ring
anchored into a tombstone.*

—RAMÓN LÓPEZ VELARDE

*You will travel, you will love, you won't get
rich. Your thirst will grow in relation to how
much you drink and how many vast oceans
you conquer.*

—VICENTE QUIRARTE

FROM THE MEXICAN NATIONAL ANTHEM

Y tus templos, palacios y torres
Se derrumben con hórrido estruendo,
Y sus ruinas existan diciendo:
De mil héroes la patria aquí fue.

¡Y retiemble en sus centros la tierra
al sonoro rugir del cañón!
¡Y retiemble en sus centros la tierra
al sonoro rugir del cañón!

And may your temples, palaces, and towers
collapse with horrid clamor
and their ruins continue on, saying:
of a thousand heroes, this country was.

And may the earth tremble at its centers
at the resounding roar of the cannon!
And may the earth tremble at its centers
at the resounding roar of the cannon!

CONTENTS

FOREWORD

RUBÉN GALLO

*A**nd Let the Earth Tremble at Its Centers* belongs to a genre with a long history in Mexican letters: the literary portrait of Mexico City. The practice began in the early sixteenth century, when the Spanish chroniclers of the Mexican conquest penned lavish descriptions of Tenochtitlan, the Aztec capital, destroyed in 1521 by a victorious Hernán Cortés. Among the ruins—toppled temples and paved canals—the Spaniards edified a new city, built from the volcanic stone known as *tezontle* that can still be seen lining the façades of the Cathedral and other grand buildings. The Spanish city was immortalized by the poet Bernardo de Balbuena, who in 1604 devoted his epic *La grandeza mexicana* [*Mexico's Grandeur*] to extolling the rich palaces and vibrant life of the first metropolis on American soil.

Literary portraits of the city blossomed after Mexico's independence from Spain in 1821. The nineteenth century saw the emergence of a new figure, the "chronicler of Mexico city," a writer who made it his mission to depict every aspect of life in the capital: the experience of walking through its streets; the flavors of its dishes;

the endless changes and metamorphoses undergone by what began as a city of canals, morphed into an elegant grid of stone palaces, and finally recast itself as a metropolis of pavement and high-rises. The first chronicler of Mexico City was Artemio de Valle Arizpe, a turn-of-the-last-century dandy who immortalized the legends and urban tales of a sleepy town that had barely reached a population of about 300,000 by 1910. The city—like the entire country—was shaken by the Revolution of 1910, but when peace was restored in 1920, a new chronicler arrived on stage: Salvador Novo, an irreverent young poet who fashioned himself as a cross between Oscar Wilde and André Gide.

An ambitious young man if there ever was one, Novo decided to rewrite Balbuena's epic ode to Mexico City, bringing it up-to-date so it could account for the numerous changes brought by the twentieth century: shiny Packards, roaring Chevrolets, and elegant Cadillacs; wide boulevards modeled after Parisian allées; art-nouveau apartment buildings and art-deco neighborhoods that were the pride of forward-looking young architects—all of these appear in Novo's 1946 *Nueva grandeza mexicana* [*New Mexican Grandeur*], a chronicle of a modern Mexico City as seen from the seat of a speeding automobile.

The next major chronicler of Mexico City was Carlos Monsiváis, an essayist who began publishing in the 1950s and has devoted his entire career to analyzing the vibrant popular culture that flourished in the capital; from the old-fashioned love songs of Agustín Lara to violent wrestling matches, from the film divas of 1950s melodramas to the macho icons of the Ranchera song, Monsiváis immortalized the most important elements of a world that no writer before him had taken seriously. His urban chronicles were collected in the volumes *Amor perdido* and *Días de guardar* and a selection was translated into English and published as *Mexican Postcards*.

As Gonzalo Celorio has written in his essay "México: Ciudad de papel" ["Mexico: City of Paper"], an English translation of which can be found in a volume I edited called *The Mexico City Reader*, the most surprising aspect of the rich literary tradition of chronicles is the fact that the Mexico City that appears in its pages is no longer there. Gone is the lake city of the Aztecs sung about by Nezahualcóyotl; gone is the "City of Palaces" immortalized by Humboldt; gone is the sparkling modern city described by Novo; even Monsiváis's city of cantinas and *lucha libre* now seems like a fading old photograph. The real city, Celorio argues, is always on the move, always reinventing itself, demolishing and reconstructing its buildings according to the latest architectural fashion; but parallel to this city of brick and mortar there is another Mexico City, a "city of paper" that lives on in the literature that has been devoted to it since the sixteenth century. "The lost city," writes Celorio in his essay, can only "be retrieved by the literature that builds it day by day, restores it, reveals it, ministers to it, and defies it" (64).

· · · · ·

Like Carlos Fuentes's classic *La región más transparente* [*Where the Air is Clear*, 1959], Celorio's *And Let the Earth Tremble at Its Centers* is a novel inspired by the long tradition of chronicles about Mexico City. But if Fuentes's novel aspires to represent the capital in its entirety—rich and poor, ancient and modern, the center and its peripheries, the autochthonous and the foreign—Celorio's focuses on only one neighborhood: "El Centro," the city's oldest quarter, home of the Cathedral and the National Palace, the main square officially called Plaza de la Constitución but affectionately called El Zócalo by virtually all of its residents. El Centro is graced by the Palace of Fine Arts, the Palace of the Inquisition, the Palace of Correos—grand constructions that once made the capital known as "the city of palaces." But many of these former mansions are now in ruins: they have been divided up into dozens of makeshift apartments in which destitute families squat; their baroque, wrought-iron balconies are now crowded with propane tanks and clothes lines; eighteenth-century stone courtyards are littered with trash; and many of these once aristocratic residences have been turned into motorcycle repair shops, taco restaurants, and, of course, bars and cantinas.

Many writers have lamented the decay of El Centro and its transformation into a neighborhood crowded by street vendors and eclectic repair shops. Historian Guillermo Tovar de Teresa, for instance, published a two-volume account of the destruction of historically significant buildings since the nineteenth century. The subtitle of his *City of Palaces* is "chronicle of a lost heritage," and the author spends every page of his study lamenting the demolition of a baroque convent, the transformation of a colonial cloister into a department store, the piercing of new avenues through the winding alleys. Dazzled by the elegance and glory of the baroque city, Tovar de Teresa can only see today's Mexico City as tragic ruin, a faint shadow of its former self.

And Let the Earth Tremble at Its Centers's portrayal of El Centro could not be more different from Tovar de Teresa's. Celorio, too, describes convents turned into shops and churches half-demolished to enlarge inner-city expressways. But rather than lamenting the loss of a glorious past, Celorio celebrates the vibrant urban life that continues to thrive in the center of Mexico City; its palaces might be in shambles and its baroque splendor might have faded, but its streets teem with vendors peddling every kind of imaginable object: from magic powders to cure evil eye to DVD players; from juicy mangos sprinkled with chili powder to the latest computer software; from t-shirts and pantsuits to wedding gowns. Amid the labyrinth of vendors and their stands, thousands of people from every imaginable social class rub shoulders: bureaucrats on their lunch break; housewives in search of the best deals; dazed visitors from the provinces; dancers clad in pseudo-Aztec attire for the amusement of American and European tourists. All one has to do is stand for a few minutes in any corner to witness the impromptu apparition of a veritable human circus.

It is this lively Mexico City—not the city of palaces but a city of people—that Celorio celebrates in *And Let the Earth Tremble at Its Centers*. The novel's protagonist, Juan Manuel Barrientos, is an erudite literature professor who also has a taste for popular culture—a happy combination of interests that makes him the perfect guide to

El Centro's nooks and crannies. As he wanders through San Juan de Letrán, Tacuba, or the alleys behind La Merced, Juan Manuel gives his readers an insider's tour of downtown Mexico City. He points out the columns of Aztec temples reused in the construction of the Cathedral; he discovers a Colonial cloister hidden behind the pink façade of an Evangelical church; he recalls the poetic names that used to grace an avenue that now bears the prosaic name of Eje Central [Central Expressway]. As he walks by these churches, convents, and palaces, Juan Manuel recalls their presence in Colonial Mexican literature: the glorious verses of Bernardo de Balbuena; the allegorical arches built on those very streets to welcome the new viceroy and immortalized by Carlos de Sigüenza y Góngora.

But Juan Manuel is not only a well-read scholar; he is also a connoisseur of the city's bars and cantinas, and his itinerary includes a tour of the neighborhood's most famous watering holes: Bar La Ópera, a once fancy establishment steps away from the Palace of Fine Arts and furnished with red velvet banquettes (to amuse tourists, waiters point to a bullet hole on the ceiling and recount the story of how, during the Revolution, Pancho Villa came for a drink and when the bill came he took out his gun and began shooting away); the legendary El Nivel, which has since closed; and many others featuring exotic or even surrealist names: La Puerta del Sol, named after one of Madrid's landmarks; Las Sirenas, which in Spanish can mean both Sirens and Mermaids (who would ever think of placing mermaids in a place with so little water and so much cement?).

One of Juan Manuel's favorite pastimes is to take his students on a tour of El Centro—an itinerary that includes palaces as well as cantinas. The professor is in his fifties; his students are in their twenties. As the novel makes clear, for most of Mexico City's younger residents—those born after 1960—El Centro is as unknown and as exotic as a foreign country. Until the 1950s, the National University was located in El Centro and its streets were crowded with students. To be a student in Mexico meant to spend several years in the neighborhood's cafés, bookstores, plazas . . . and bars. But once the University relocated to the vast modernist campus designed by Mario Pani and his team of architects on the southern edge of the city, El Centro lost its students and young people lost contact with one of the city's most dynamic neighborhoods. Juan Manuel's students were born in the suburbs, and their daily routine involves crisscrossing the city from north to south, from east to west, driving along the expressways built in the 1950s and 1960s and designed to bypass the crowded central neighborhoods.

· · · · ·

The title of the novel, *And Let the Earth Tremble at Its Centers*, is a verse from the Mexican national anthem, composed by Francisco González Bocanegra after Mexico obtained its independence from Spain in 1821. The anthem's lyrics are as bellicose as befits a nation emerging from a prolonged war:

> *¡Mexicanos! al grito de guerra*
> *El acero aprestad y el bridón*
> *Y retiemble en sus centros la tierra*
> *Al sonoro rugir del cañón.*
> *[...]*
> *Más si osare un extraño enemigo*
> *Profanar con su planta tu suelo,*
> *Piensa, ¡oh Patria querida! que el cielo*
> *Un soldado en cada hijo te dio.*

> [Mexicans! At the cry of war
> Ready your swords and the horses
> And may the earth tremble at its centers
> At the canon's thundering roar

> And if ever a foreign enemy
> Dared to trample your land
> Think, oh motherland! that heaven
> Gave you a soldier in every one of your sons.]

To this day Mexican schools have their students perform an elaborate ritual in honor of the flag every Monday morning: boys and girls sing the anthem, salute the flag, and march around the schoolyard imitating the strut of military marches. Every schoolboy knows the anthem's lyrics by heart, even if the precise meaning of those bellicose utterances escapes him. There is even an old joke about the anthem's arcane language: a young peasant woman has just given birth; when the priest asks her what name she will give the boy she answers he will be called Masiosare. "Masiosare?" retorts the priest, "I've never heard such a name." "It's in the national anthem," the woman chirps back, "You know: the name of the foreign enemy, Masiosare, *un extraño enemigo.*"

The novel gets its title from another pun on the national anthem. Wandering through the streets of El Centro, Juan Manuel recalls the verse *"y retiemble en sus centros la tierra."* What would happen, he wonders, if one took the bellicose verse and made *"sus centros"* refer not to the bowels of the earth but to the center of Mexico City? What would it mean for downtown to tremble? (El Centro did indeed tremble during the tragic earthquake of 1985, when dozens of tall buildings tumbled, trapping or killing tens of thousands of its residents). Lost in his associations, Juan Manuel remembers a curious detail about national history that will become important for the novel: in his original version of the anthem, the composer did not write *"centros"* but *"antros"*—a word stemming from the same etymology as the English term "entrails," but which has acquired an altogether different meaning in colloquial Mexican Spanish. An *"antro"* is a dive, a hole in the wall, a sleazy bar. And since Juan Manuel's tour of El Centro is also a tour of its *antros*, the anthem does poetic justice to the reality of downtown Mexico City. The center of the city trembles with people, with vendors, with crowds; and nowhere does it tremble as intensely and as violently as inside its rowdy cantinas. It is precisely the story of that trembling—that minor earthquake of Mexico City's nightlife— that Celorio's novel recounts.

· · · · ·

And Let the Earth Tremble at Its Centers is not only a novel about El Centro; it is also an inventive bildungsroman. Through a series of flashbacks—induced by beer, tequila, and other cocktails imbibed along the way—Juan Manuel evokes important moments of his childhood and adolescence: his first drink, during a weekend visit to his friend's Cuernavaca house; the death of his father; a formative trip to the northern city of Matehuala to stay with his half-brother Ángel; his initiation into the mysteries of sexuality in a dusty motel owned by an ex-pat named Mr. Prince.

Celorio has used a similar narrative technique in his other novels, most recently in *Tres lindas cubanas* [*Three Pretty Cuban Girls*], his most ambitious work to date, recounting the history of his Cuban-Mexican family and his three trips to Havana, before and after the generalized disenchantment with the Cuban Revolution. The novel narrates the story of three generations of his mother's family through a series of flashbacks and childhood memories.

In *And Let the Earth Tremble at Its Centers*, Juan Manuel's memories point to the evolution of Mexico City from the 1950s until the present. During his boyhood years, the city still had the atmosphere of a provincial town: its streets were lined with trees, a handful of American automobiles cruised down its boulevards, and the air was still clear. In the decades that followed, the population exploded, the city received a massive influx of migrants from the countryside, and gradually cement and smog smothered its streets. The novel opens in a chaotic Mexico City, an eternally congested megalopolis that forces Juan Manuel to spend time in his car, traversing the city from south to north to get from the university to El Centro.

Along with the population and the cityscape, Mexico City's famous nightlife underwent a radical transformation from the 1950s to the present. Juan Manuel recalls how as a little boy he used to walk by La Fuente, the famous cabaret where the legendary diva Ana Bertha Lepe performed risqué shows wearing—as the ads proclaimed—"10 ounces of clothes." The 1950s were the glory days of the cabaret—that Mexican institution immortalized by Ninón Sevilla in the film *Aventurera*. In these establishments, men could pay to dance with one of the many women working the floor: one simply had to buy a *ficha*, a token, for the privilege of sharing a song with the pretty *fichera*, as these dancing women were known. The interactions between these mostly married men and *ficheras* were governed by an unspoken code of honor and civility. Gentlemen paid for the privilege of dancing, talking, perhaps holding hands, but no more. . . . The *fichera* was a lady and she had to be treated as such.

During the 1960s and the 1970s the sexual revolution brought profound changes to Mexico City's nightlife: the first gay bar opened in a discrete basement in Zona Rosa; the first American-style discos appeared in the city; and rock music, sung in Spanish, made the city's entrails tremble. The 1980s brought karaoke bars and other foreign imports. But it was the 1990s that brought the most radical transformation to the capital's nightlife.

During most of the seventy years that the Institutional Revolutionary Party (PRI) ruled Mexico, the government kept tight controls on the city's nightlife. Health inspectors roamed bars and cabarets, and would shutter an establishment in no time if they considered the unspoken code of decency had been broken. But these rules were liberalized in the 1990s during the presidency of Carlos Salinas; after the signature of the North American Free Trade Agreement, nightlife got wilder. It was then that the famous "table dance" bars began sprouting like mushrooms throughout the city. No more honor code, no more quaint notions of chivalry or respect; these new places advertised, quite openly, sex for sale.

The last bar Juan Manuel visits during his *noche de ronda* is one of these tables, as the establishments are affectionately known in Mexico City. Readers witness the shock felt by this old-fashioned scholar, used to cantinas and cabarets, upon entering the table of iniquity. As in the old days, there are still tokens, but it is no longer possible to dance with a partner; instead, a topless woman wearing a G-string will come to the table and dance on the paying gentle-man. "You can touch any part of her, except the genitals. And if you purchase three tickets, you can go with her to a private room, where she'll dance three songs, just for you, but completely naked this time."

The rise of tables in Mexico City dealt the deathblow to the last remaining cabarets. Presented with the choice of either danc-ing with or being danced on, male patrons opted for the latter. In those same years, the capital was shaken again by an unprecedented crime wave. The Salinas boom years came to an abrupt end in 1995, when one of the most severe economic crises in the history of the country plunged Mexico City into an abyss; the peso tumbled, interest rates soared, and millions of middle-class Mexicans lost their jobs, their cars and their homes. There was an explosion of violent crimes: robberies, burglaries, kidnappings, and even mur-ders. Mexico City became one of the most dangerous places on the planet, and going out at night now included the added thrill of anticipating thefts or kidnappings. In the first pages of the novel we see Juan Manuel preparing to leave his house and deciding to leave his credit cards at home . . . just in case he falls victim to an "express kidnapping," a misdeed consisting of driving the hap-less victim to a cash machine and holding a gun to his head until he has withdrawn all available funds. We learn that Juan Manuel "didn't know the access codes anyway, which could be fatal in the event of a mugging."

It is no coincidence that Juan Manuel's night out turns sour at the table dancing club—and not at any of the dozen or so tradi-tional cantinas he visits before. The rise of tables was part of the gangsterization of Mexico City—and it is inside this seedy estab-lishment that a drunk Juan Manuel is robbed of all his belongings by a gang of thugs sporting police uniforms.

In the end, the death of Juan Manuel represents the death of a period in the history of Mexico City—a time when it was safe to walk the streets of El Centro, to hop from one cantina to another and visit one or two cabarets along the way. The city that Juan Manuel loved to share with his students is rapidly turning into another "city of paper," yet another one of the many aspects of city life that have ceased to exist, except in the pages of its novelists, poets, and chroniclers.

El Nivel is now closed. How long will Las Sirenas, La Puerta del Sol, or La Ópera remain open? But Celorio, unlike Tovar de Teresa, does not lament the ever-changing nature of Mexico City. *And Let the Earth Tremble at Its Centers* is not a nostalgic novel; it is a realist work that faithfully represents the never-ending metamorphoses undergone by the city. At least since 1521, the Mexican capital has never ceased to reinvent itself. It vanished as a city of canals to reemerge as a city of stone buildings; its baroque palaces changed façades in the nineteenth century to adopt the more fashionable neoclassical style; the quaint provincial city of 1900 was reborn as a bustling megalopolis around 1950; and the Mexico City portrayed in Celorio's novel—with its cantinas, its cabarets, its tropical music—has now been replaced by a globalized urban center where hip kids dance to the beats of techno music—sung in English, Spanish, French, or German.

· · · · ·

And Let the Earth Tremble at Its Centers leaves us with an apocalyptic vision of Mexico City as a place in which going out for a drink can turn into a deadly trap. The novel's dark ending reminds the reader of a paradox that Juan Villoro—another avid chronicler of the capital's popular culture—has explored in his essay, "The Metro," which also appears in English in *The Mexico City Reader*. Why, he asks, isn't there a mass exodus from Mexico City? Its inhabitants have made it a sport to lament the many plagues that have descended on the capital: poverty, overcrowding, traffic jams, pollution, violence, corruption. But if things are so bad, why do people stay? Villoro finds the answer to this puzzling question in an opera by Stravinsky. Mexico City's residents, he argues, are like that character in *The Rake's Progress* who falls in love with a bearded

lady at the circus. She might be hideous, overweight, and hairy
. . . but love is blind. And the same has happened to Mexico City's
residents, who continue to love, despite their frequent complaints,
their smog-filled and crime-ridden hometown. *And Let the Earth
Tremble at Its Centers* is one more family portrait of this hirsute
but lovable urban hag.

———

AND
LET THE
EARTH
TREMBLE
AT ITS
CENTERS

———

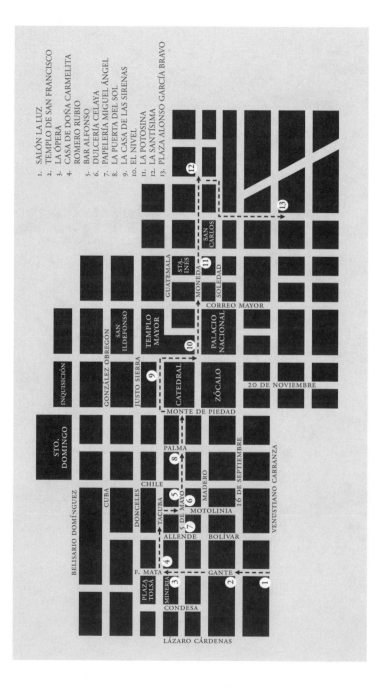

CHAPTER 1

THAT MORNING, Dr. Juan Manuel Barrientos didn't write a single word. He didn't drink his usual cup of coffee that magically transported him from sleep to writing. He didn't play the customary choral music either. For him, it was a strangely quiet morning.

Still half asleep, he winced when he remembered that slobbery, fetid kiss still stuck to his cheek. The saliva in his mouth tasted bitter. He looked pale. He felt nauseous. His head was hurting, and his back was hurting, too, as if he had been flogged. And his knees hurt.

He couldn't remember anything that had happened the night before. Only a few disconnected, blurry images came to mind. Everyone there had ended up falling asleep. You, Juan Manuel, were the only one who stayed awake. That part you do remember, as well as some of the things you pondered while the others were sleeping, stretched out anywhere and however they could. But who knows how the hell you made it to your bedroom, because you're in your bedroom and in your own bed. Like gauze to a wound, he could feel his eyelids stuck together. It was painful to open them, and all he saw was the luminous slit between the curtains. It was Friday morning. It's Friday morning, Juan Manuel. You've got an appointment today. At noon. Downtown. And the Friday traffic. He felt his way to the dresser, searching for his glasses. Luckily, he found them. It was 7:25 a.m. Seven and twenty-five makes thirty-two, he thought, as if his primary school teacher was testing his addition skills.

He didn't want to go. Even if he had been feeling better, he still had no desire to go. It certainly wasn't the same desire that he had expressed the day before, because he had acceded to their request with euphoria. And now that's what it had become—an obligation. It always turned out that way: first the passion, then the sacrifice, which is the flip side of passion, a perfect opposite.

While still in bed, he picked up the phone and tried calling Antonio. No answer.

It was hard for him to get out of bed. He hadn't slept much, and he had a hangover. Nevertheless, his sense of discipline was stronger than how he was feeling. He couldn't just cancel on them. Besides, he needed to swing by the university, if only for a couple of hours.

His urine flowed dark yellow. Unable to look at himself in the mirror, he brushed his teeth with his eyes closed. Then he gulped as much water as he could from the faucet. He made no attempt to do his standard sixteen minutes on the stationary bike; instead, he remained in the shower much longer than usual, letting the hot water massage him as it flowed from the showerhead. Hoping to remove what felt like thorns stuck into his temples and the nape of his neck, he meticulously washed his hair. Stroking his eyelids and left cheek, which was hurting him, he delicately washed his face. Who was he? Who was that guy who came out of nowhere and planted a kiss on his cheek? He had no idea who he was. He had never seen him before.

Intuiting that perhaps tonight might be the last time he would use them, Juan Manuel was especially attentive about washing his male parts. Hoping to restore any lost energy, he finished showering with icy-cold water, even though he was barely able to stand it a few seconds that seemed more like several minutes. Now chilled, he used gymnastic vigor to dry his hair and the rest of his body. Then he started coughing almost to the point of vomiting. After getting out of the shower, he wiped the steam from the mirror with a towel and, despite the refreshing water, he discovered a sorry-looking figure—bloodshot eyes with dark circles under them, sagging cheeks, a graying beard. After shaving with an unsteady hand, he sloshed a more-than-usual amount of cologne on his face, temples, and neck.

As he gave himself a last sympathetic glance in the mirror, a fleeting image of Jimena and her feline nose crossed his line of vision.

Hoping to counter the feeling of collapse and in some way restore some energy, he dressed meticulously, choosing clothes that should have stimulated his now-spent jovial spirit. But, Juan Manuel, if you could only see that, instead of rejuvenating you, it only made you look older. He put on a treasured pair of faded, ragged jeans, argyle socks, dark-red Italian loafers, an audacious tie that contrasted with his dark shirt, and one of his lightest ancestral tweed blazers, because, despite the grayish days lately, the weather had been unusually warm.

If, at this very moment, you were to discover a cadaver in your closet, whom would you call, Juan Manuel? Yes, the body of a young man sprawled out on the floor underneath your suits neatly hung in plastic bags? With an extended arm seemingly grasping for help, blood would have been trickling from the corner of his mouth with his eyes wide open, staring at nothing. So, whom would you call?

He clumsily gathered up his personal effects that were scattered about the room—glasses, watch, red kerchief, address book, keys, and pens. He took his credit cards from his wallet and placed them in a drawer. Why take chances on losing them? Besides, he had plenty of cash. And he didn't know the PINs, which could be fatal in the event of a mugging. He stuck two Maalox tablets in his shirt pocket and, despite the disgust he felt at that moment, he placed a Montecristo cigar, which he would enjoy later, in the outside pocket of his coat. He opened a drawer and took out his silver hip flask bearing the initials J.M.B.A., which contained tequila for that unexpected moment, and put it into his rear hip pocket. An umbrella: the weather had been fickle lately and you never know.

He went down the stairs and found the place in ruins. Everybody had gone home, but the vestiges of those who had been there the night before were in plain sight: dirty glasses; ashtrays crammed with cigarette butts; long-play records here and there. He closed his eyes. I wish Baldomera would come, he thought.

So, barely managing to cloak the havoc done to him and ignoring the disaster done to his house the night before, he strategically placed his paraphernalia in the corresponding pockets of his shirt, blazer, and pants, after which he left for the university. Although he felt somewhat revived, he looked like hell. You can always shake off a hangover, Juan Manuel, but it's impossible to disguise it.

Before getting into his car, he walked down to the corner juice vendor, who concocted a shot of Tres Coronas sherry with a two-yolk chaser. That combo settled his stomach a bit, although at that moment he was either about to heave or slowly begin to accept the shot of alcohol. You can feel your eyelids begin to perspire, and you can even hear the voice of an angel, which is what they all say, as a group of men stood in front of the juice stand, initiating their day with that hangover cure.

The morning was gray and polluted, like almost every morning in the city. The sun wasn't capable of penetrating the scum that hung over the valley like a gigantic cataplasm. The few rays that did manage to get through only intensified the filthy air, which was composed of toxic ingredients, haze, and desolation. Reduced to a snail's pace in the heavy traffic, thousands of cars were lined up heading south on the beltway, while many, many more made their way north, which isn't entirely true, because they had come to a complete standstill. It was that time of day when children carrying enormous backpacks of useless school supplies were going to school, and office workers were making their way to work with the stress of time clocks on their faces. After finally getting onto the beltway, he saw the university come into view. At that early hour, the campus seemed like a luminous green island in the middle of a turbulent, agitated urban ocean.

At the university, Dr. Barrientos did little more than satisfy his customary obsession of being punctual, an obligation that he had imposed upon himself to thwart any self-recriminations. He tried reaching Antonio on the phone, threw some junk mail into the trash basket, and cancelled an invitation to attend a meeting of Mexican scholars in Austin, Texas. Despite his irritated eyes and headache, he detected—as if it were a fly dropping—a typographical error that soiled the first page of his recently published article on architecture and poetry of the allegorical arches of New Spain.

He tried reaching Antonio a third time, but still no one answered.

In order to meet his students downtown, he would have to leave by 11:00 a.m., which was about the time of day when the daily routine in his department had already started to wind down, leaving the place a tomb by early afternoon. He told the secretary that he'd be back on Monday.

Refusing to have to think about choosing alternate routes, he decided to cross the city using Insurgentes Avenue. Neither the sherry nor the water he had consumed had quenched his thirst. Even though the hour was propitious for less traffic, cars were moving slowly. In truth, Insurgentes had become an architectural chaos of fake renovations that pained Dr. Barrientos. In the southern part of the city, trees that had once surrounded country homes at the beginning of the past century and now shielded restaurants and boutiques had thinned out around the Viaduct. Back then, you still hadn't taken a physics class. You had just started junior high, and you were poor in math. You didn't understand weights and measurements—well, measurements perhaps. For instance, you could calculate the number of steps between the classroom door and the flagpole outside. Even though you might fudge a bit as you got closer to the pole by taking greater strides or smaller steps to conform to your guess, you were almost always right. But how could you imagine the weight of one pound, such as a pound in the abstract sense? If a pound of bronze was the size of a particular weight on a scale, then a pound of feathers had to be huge, like the elongated pillow on your parents' bed. Even so, you still assumed that a pound of feathers could never weigh the same as a pound of bronze. And if you were unable to imagine the weight of one pound, it was even more difficult to think about an ounce—or several ounces—of something. Like an ounce of clothing, for instance. Taking a window seat on the school bus, you would wait anxiously to pass by La Fuente, a nightclub just before the Viaduct, where Ana Bertha Lepe was always waiting for you. Practically naked, she was wearing something transparent over her nipples and her crotch. You calculated that she would have been fourteen strides tall . . . if you could have climbed her to the top, starting with those marvelous calves, then shinnying up her thighs, scaling her large breasts, finally reaching her puffy, erotic lips and staring into her fiery eyes. The gigantic figure completely blocked La Fuente from view, but there was an enormous sign on top of the building—ANA BERTHA LEPE, ONLY AN OUNCE OF CLOTHING. And the bus would speed up, preventing you from running your eyes up and down that monumental body, making your temples pound, your heart pulsate, and your groin hot. One time after getting home from school, you asked your mother how much an ounce was. Do you have cobwebs in your head? An ounce of what? he wondered, as she beat some eggs for a dessert. Just an ounce, you thought. It's about three acorns, she replied. And while you strategically placed each one on Ana Bertha Lepe's body, you suddenly felt like something was going to explode in your pants. Once past the Viaduct, back then the pavement came to an end, giving way to an area of flimsy, makeshift housing that had popped up haphazardly after an earthquake had devastated the Roma neighborhood in the city. But today, given the sudden heat of the day, the conglomeration of cars, bottlenecks, corner vendors, street urchins washing windshields at each light, and clowns breathing fire along the roadway had made you so irritable that you almost stop your car right there at Cuauhtémoc Monument, jump out, and run away from it all.

I know! A beer, but under the shade of a straw hut on Mandinga Lake in Veracruz! For the love of God, just a beer! He continued down Reforma Avenue and turned on Juárez. Only skeletons of buildings were left from a bygone era of opulence. Empty lots in the midst of an enormous population. Scaffolding, construction trenches, and electric wires were everywhere.

"These [ruins], Fabius—oh, how painful!—that you see now . . ."

He parked his car at the Palace of Fine Arts. If only for a few minutes, he felt liberated from the prison of the automobile, but then he became engulfed in a sea of pedestrians scurrying in every direction imaginable. Crossing Lázaro Cárdenas Circle, an arterial road which you still prefer to call San Juan de Letrán, he turned down Tacuba. Reaching Filomeno Mata, he crossed Cinco de Mayo at the block where the street changed its name to Gante, and continued past Madero to Dieciséis de Septiembre. As if his appointment were in London and not in Mexico City, he stood in front of Salón La Luz at exactly noon.

It had been a while since he'd been to that bar. You remembered that at one time the place was in the basement, or at least below street level. You also remembered that it used to be dark inside, but who knows if that was true, or if your memory was fading. Back then, it was a bar only for men, all kinds of men, the type of which had become scarce, because in those clandestine surroundings you could actually drink 96-proof alcohol from bottles in brown paper bags. Nowadays, these bars—once the sole domain of men—were also open to women. This place had been transformed into something like a European bar. There were round tables with large umbrellas on the sidewalk in front and green foliage in massive clay pots.

None of the students had arrived yet. He started to get irritated. Even though he always ended up waiting for other people, he was always punctual. It occurred to him to walk around a bit until everyone showed up, which would be in keeping with his age, status, and the sacrifice he had made to get there, considering how lousy he felt. But he stopped and turned around. Besides, he needed a beer. Even though it was just a bar and the white tablecloths had already been placed on the tables, for most people it was still too early to have a drink. There was nary a customer inside. The floor had been mopped, the waiters were getting ready to open—cutting limes for shots of tequila, peeling shrimp, chopping onions, and carving up chickens for the soup that was the specialty of the restaurant, whose founder, Lencho, later used the same recipe at La Providencia, in San Ángel, where, by the way, during the mundane act of slicing up a loaf of rye bread, he whacked off three fingers of his left hand.

He decided to sit down in one of those outdoor rustic chairs and wait for the culinary frenzy inside to slow down before ordering a beer.

A block of ice had just been delivered to the restaurant and, having been placed on the sidewalk, it started to melt and trickle into the street. A merciful waiter finally brought out a beer, even though it still wasn't quite cold enough. Nevertheless, he took a long swig, which made him feel as good as the shower he had taken earlier in the day. The beer gave him momentary relief, and he capped it off with a slight burp. You really don't know how important beer can be until you need one.

Where's Antonio? Why wouldn't he answer the phone? Has he backed out on me?

All around him, the rest of the world was going about its business. Briefcase-laden bureaucrats, pot-bellied merchants, and hardworking people were scurrying around everywhere. While a blind man rattled a tambourine nearby, a street urchin tried to sell him some lottery tickets . . . c'mon, just one, just one, don't be mean . . . see? You are. When Barrientos shook his head, the little boy changed tactics and begged for money to buy a taco. With the same decisive slap as a flyswatter, he said "No!"

Yesterday, he had met with his students at Casa Pedro to celebrate the end of the semester. He had taught a class on relationships between baroque literature and New Spain's architecture. His head still pounded from the raucous laughter triggered by rounds and rounds of beer and shots of tequila. Even though the world of academia had been briefly displaced by bursts of gratification, its presence was never totally absent, because it could be felt through the growing delirium of erudite references, puns, irony, and jokes, some of which were almost indecipherable. It was as if literary greats like Baltasar Gracián, Luis de Góngora, Carlos de Sigüenza y Góngora, and Sor Juana Inés de la Cruz had been invited to join them. However, following the baroque tradition of deflection, the euphoria within which everyone was submerged had created anything but joy and happiness; instead, there was the need to conceal a general feeling of sadness, the need to feel the sorrow coming at the end of his course, because you, Dr. Barrientos, had announced your retirement. No, you won't be teaching anymore, which is what you've done for the past twenty-five years. Suddenly, overtaking the rowdiness in the restaurant, silence quickly spread throughout, as if one of those present were about to stand up and give a serious speech. On the tables, gold and silver, beer and tequila. In a moment of suspense, all eyes turned to you, yes, to you, Juan Manuel. You took a long and solemn swig of beer after which, devoutly, you put a dash of salt on a slice of lime and, holding the jigger of tequila with two fingers—your index and your thumb—you raised it in homage to your faithful followers, your students. You downed it in one swallow, right to the last drop without savoring its flavor on your tongue, but only after which you sonorously exhaled the aftereffects of the salt and lime. Quivering slightly, you looked at your disciples one by one and told them with a smile that despite your retirement you would always be there for them: I'm leaving, but somehow, I'll always be nearby. Precisely at that moment, you accepted their invitation to meet them today, which is exactly what you're doing right now. Fernando suggested it, and Jimena enthusiastically endorsed the idea. Ah, Jimena. Her feline profile, whose nose corroborates each word she speaks, possessed that unique gesture that you desire to capture, detain, and protect, allowing you forever to re-create and possess it. As night approached in that southern part of the city where unpaved streets were spotted with brackish pools of water, you invited your students to your house to continue partying and celebrating your retirement. However, it was impossible to make it last. The euphoria of the moment had disappeared with the interruption of having to leave one place and go to another, where everything was different—the light, the temperature, everything. No matter, when the restaurant closed the bar, you implored your students to follow you home to have one last drink. You desperately wanted to rekindle that pleasure of listening to some of your best bolero songs and those unsuspecting tunes. By then, however, everyone was drained and sleepy. Conversations became fragmented. No one was laughing like before. Everything had become stultified. Lingering murmurs turned silent. While Bola de Nieve ripped into in the song he was singing on the record player, people were yawning. Catalina and Patricia left first. You turned sad when Fernando left with Jimena, cutting short the possibility of hooking up with her that night. So, what would have happened anyway, Juan Manuel? Perhaps you would have become aroused and found the right words to seduce her, but more than likely, you would have engulfed her in your sadness and ended up frustrated. Besides, you wouldn't have been able to make love to her. You were drunk, and, given her youthful beauty, you would have been embarrassed by your flabby arms and voluminous gut. You're some twenty-five years older than she is, which translates to the same number of years that you had been the head of the department since your graduation. Incredible! Héctor, Julia, Susana, and Antonio, of course, had agreed to stay a while longer, but like the others they were already dozing off or talking among themselves. Suddenly, you found yourself alone, catching a whiff of an unfinished cigar, hardly differentiating between the scotch—without ice—that you were consuming at home and the rounds of tequila that you had downed at the restaurant, listening to the energetic, sometimes clamorous, yet subtle sigh of Bola de Nieve's piano and scrutinizing your tall bookshelves. Exhausted, you were lost in the rapture of the music. You had reached the end of the line. Your sense of discipline could no longer counter the feeling of surrender. And now that you were retired, you were ready to let go. You were dead on your feet.

You couldn't remember if you had fallen asleep when that wicked-looking, idiotic young man with the greasy hair and toothless smile showed up at your place and gave you a kiss on the cheek. Your students had already fallen asleep on the couches in your study. You can't remember anything else. Apparently, Antonio woke up and sent the intruder packing. Without asking permission, the guy poured himself a drink and peed in a flowerpot on the porch. Antonio pushed him out the door, and that's the last you remember.

Lugging a small, brightly painted wooden box belonging to a Roman circus and sporting numerous colorful thumbtacks, tiny mirrors, and pictures of famous boxers, a shoeshine boy approached, distracting you from your fragmented memories. Need a shine, young man? he asked. Your Italian loafers didn't need it, but you said yes, if only to kill some time while you waited. They should have arrived before you.

With sacrosanct devotion to his trade, the shoeshine boy begins first by placing his equipment on the sidewalk in orderly fashion. Next, he inserts pieces of leather between your shoes and your socks, so as not to stain them. Then he soaps up your shoes with hygienic fervor in order to proceed with the actual shoeshine itself. It was like a religious liturgy, and you scrutinized his every move. He daubs a rag carefully wrapped around two fingers with oxblood wax and applies it to each shoe. Then comes a first pass with the brush without making them glisten yet. Next, he applies a neutral-colored wax directly with his fingers. Applying the brush a second time, but much more vigorously, it feels like he's going to massage your feet, Juan Manuel, appreciatively. Finally, he unrolls a strip of cloth to buff your shoes, and with five snapping sounds in the air before a light going-over, as if he were dusting off priceless pieces of jewelry, he gives three light taps on the sides of the soles of your shoes to let you know the ritual has ended.

Somehow, you feel purified. For a moment, you think that that if you were poor you wouldn't mind being a shoeshine boy, because in barely three minutes he can produce a veritable work of art, even if the results are somewhat pedestrian. Faintly smiling, with that adjective you recognize the opportune precision of your choice of words and see in yourself something of a priest conducting the rights of initiation—shining your disciples' shoes. Oh, Juan Manuel, it's amazing how a hangover can make us ever so humble!

Partially hidden by the potted shrubs from the stares of a growing number of people who were passing by on their way to work, you took a last swig of your beer.

Then you glanced at your watch. Twelve after twelve, you mutter, with defiant resignation. That adds up to twenty-four. What begins badly, ends badly. The ten-minute grace period was over, so if they don't arrive by fifteen after, you'll have to order another beer—now colder—despite the fact that you'll be violating the first rule of the game, that is, not to have more than one drink at each bar. Otherwise, staying in one bar entraps your inebriated soul, and you end up in a process of confession, arguments, and then reconciliation. Hence, it's important to get out of the bar and seek renewal. Actually, this is a self-imposed decision to prevent you from getting drunk too soon. However, once you've had two or three shots of tequila by three o'clock and feelings of condescension are taking over, you'll have already violated your own rules. By imposing that early morning discipline upon yourself, you've only created a ploy for not going off the deep end; or it could be the other way around: the laxity that begins to overtake you in the early afternoon is simply a tactic for responding to your desire to defy the rigidity of your self-imposed discipline. Do you really believe that slacking off in the afternoons is your reward for the applied rigor of your work in the mornings? Or is your severity a way of chastising yourself for your excesses of the night before?

The planned excursion was neither an excuse for barhopping nor a formal class on architecture, but rather a melding of the two that was driven by the personality of Juan Manuel Barrientos. Guided by the erudition found in libraries and specialized archives and based on interminable walking tours, he became familiar with all the streets and plazas of downtown Mexico City. He had studied the inner city's civil and religious buildings, its shifting history, super-positions, aberrant alterations, and inconceivable destruction. But he also knew the bars, the dives, the local joints, the holes-in-the-wall, and the downtrodden places that sought to maintain some of their historical dignity. On the one hand, Juan Manuel accepted the invitation with enthusiasm, because it was a forum that he could continue to dominate outside the classroom as a way to hold sway over those students who had made him feel so young and alive. On the other hand, he was a little apprehensive about the whole thing, mainly because he knew only too well that his explanations about architecture would eventually become saturated with alcohol. Although he has long known his limits, his tolerance has been greatly reduced over time. In addition, you were extremely annoyed about feeling panicky, because you woke up this morning feeling like hell, and in your efforts to normalize things, you could very well go off the deep end. But there's no going back now, Juan Manuel.

Antonio, his most advanced disciple and teaching assistant, had agreed to organize the excursion suggested by Fernando and supported by Jimena's enthusiasm. He was absolutely positive that they were supposed to meet at Salón La Luz at noon sharp. We'll see you at Salón La Luz at noon tomorrow, said Antonio as he was leaving Juan Manuel's house, after having thrown out the party crasher and said good-bye to his classmates, who had already fallen asleep. Finally, now, he remembered it all perfectly.

He glanced at his watch again. It was 12:15 p.m. What the hell, I'll order another beer. It's not your fault.

You don't miss your other students—Antonio, Fernando, Héctor, Javier—the way you miss Jimena. You more than like her. You're enchanted by her feline gestures and the way her words and smile transform her nose. She would send you into a frenzy with that raspy voice; even if you believed that you didn't like her that much, her presence would always be necessary. The presence of women has always fascinated you. Somehow, they modify your behavior and transform your conversations. It would take only one woman—

just one—to be present for you to feel the impulse to seduce her, if only verbally.

Now it was 12:30 p.m. Taking the last sip of his second beer, he knew that his disciples weren't coming. What a waste, he thought, and then he felt that slobbery kiss on his cheek. If you were to discover a cadaver in your closet, Juan Manuel, whom would you call? Just whom would you call?

He had the option of returning home, but it took him longer just to consider that option than it did to reject the idea outright, because there was the traffic, the dirty glasses, the filthy plates, the ashtrays full of cigarette butts, and the stench of unfinished cigars. And it was highly unlikely that Baldomera had shown up to clean the house today. And to top it off, spending an afternoon at home depressed him. All he would do was sleep three hours, wake up in a bad humor not wanting to do anything, and face a sleepless night. Instead, he needed a stronger drink right now. He decided to do the tour by himself. Well, truth be told, he didn't make that decision himself. It was a sentence that had to be obeyed to its fullest extent.

He decided to leave the bar and paid the bill. With two midday beers under his belt, he felt a certain effervescence bubbling in his head. He exited the green demarcation line of Salón La Luz, and, despite the dirty air surrounding him, he walked into the luminosity of early afternoon. It was so sunny that afternoon that, as soon as the professor became integrated into the pedestrian traffic, his umbrella became a teacher's pointer, as if his students were following him. He pointed out a frieze here, a cornice there, and spires and archivolts. He was taking no fixed route, because the second rule of the game that he had imposed upon himself consisted of not following any preconceived itinerary or taking any predetermined route, but only of respecting his intuition and even his tottering.

CHAPTER 2

Walking up Gante Street, Juan Manuel came upon the Methodist church and its Disneyland-like façade, which concealed the main cloister of the old San Francisco Convent. During the time of the viceroyalty, that colossal edifice was originally some type of fortress right in the middle of that enormous open space next to the main plaza. And during the reform period after the republican years of the nineteenth century, it was dismembered. If it wasn't practically destroyed outright, the building complex had been pillaged, modified, or adapted for new purposes and destinies. Little remains of the original convent; only vestiges linger that are now dispersed among more modern buildings that have sprung up on the original site, such as San Francisco Church, which has been rebuilt over time due to fires. Today, you enter the church from Madero Street, not San Juan de Letrán, where you find the original main entrance, now blocked by stores and encroaching buildings. Looking like a hermitage, the Chapel of San Antonio is on the far side of a cemetery (belonging to a religious order) that for many years was left abandoned by the city. The chapel itself has long been falling apart, now a giant specter receiving light through growing cracks and crevices. There are other remnants of this complex, now spread about here and there, such as the small, intimate service cloister located today inside the Ideal Bakery, where you can see a piece of the arch of a portal through which pilgrims would pass, still miraculously intact despite earthquakes. And directly in front of you finally, this cloistered cloister that was acquired by a Protestant group that had the good sense to protect the church as if they had placed it inside a bell jar.

Since the temple door was ajar, Dr. Barrientos walked in with a professorial air about him, only to find a glum custodian in the vestibule. The professor whispered a devotional prayer that could barely be heard so as not to reveal the smell of beer on his breath. He continued inside the magnificent cloister that was hidden by that façade outside. The imagery with which the Counter-Reformation attempted to ward off the fear of an immense void that had underlain and motivated the Baroque had been substituted by music and singing under the guise of Protestantism. Using some examples that didn't exactly coincide with his state of mind, that is what Dr. Barrientos would have told his students had they come along. He was concerned about his headache, among other things. Despite those benign beers, it wouldn't go away.

Upon entering the building, Juan Manuel could hear a choir singing its praises to the Lord. It was composed of men and women of different ages, whose musical vocation or piety wouldn't be evident if they had been singing somewhere else.

Jimena was astonished. She never would have thought that behind that rose-colored façade there would be an enclosure so beautiful, yet so solemn. Juan Manuel smiled, stimulated by the surprise that he had triggered in his student. He invited her to sit down next to him in a pew in order to absorb the beauty of the cloister—its dancing arches, the architectural resolution of each corner, and the sixteenth-century Plateresque ornamentation. As these things were pointed out to her, they were described in a low voice, not so much to avoid distracting those early afternoon singers as to justify placing his lips ever so close to her ear and the soft peach fuzz on her earlobe.

He had always enjoyed choral music, the earlier in the morning, the better. He was used to getting up at sunrise every day in order to write, and he would always play some type of religious music; conversely, after a few drinks in the evening, when his erudition had evaporated, he was also capable of listening to and singing popular jukebox songs. He was surprised by the enjoyment he got from listening to canticles dedicated to the Virgin Mary, or Gregorian chants sung before and after the reading of the psalms. To hear them was to recuperate his lost faith, or at least he could re-create the serenity and wholeness that religious faith had meant to him when he was a child and long before those inner voices began tormenting him with frightening questions, such as what did God do in order to become God, the time before blasphemy uncontrollably and irrepressibly dirtied his young lips in that ever-so-small San Sebastián Church in Chimalistac, where you went to Mass every Sunday with your mother and sister Adela. Not only due to their saintly devotion, but also because of the stimulation you received from the organ music and the celestial voices of the choir, you felt simultaneously the plenitude of grace and the fear of losing it. At that supreme moment, when your soul was summoned by angels to appear before the Virgin Mary, who from her golden throne was enveloped in fluffy clouds, she smiled maternally at you; but a voice deep inside you uttered an astoundingly insolent remark: fucking-virginmarywhore. You attempted to muzzle that voice coming from within you, honest, Mother Mary, I didn't say that, because I love you and I promise that . . . Don't be stupid, dumb ass, interrupted that little voice, reeling off all the dirty words you had learned with embarrassment from your older classmates, who were always quarreling with everyone. It was true: listening to religious music every morning enabled you to erase the human excesses from the night before and to submit yourself to a process of purification not unlike the shoe shine you had just received. That pious chanting had embellished the San Francisco cloister and spirited you away.

· · · · ·

You were fourteen years old, Juan Manuel, and you were about to finish junior high. You were celebrating your birthday at Uriarte's summer home in Cuernavaca. He was only a few months older than you, but he was a lot taller, bigger, and wiser. Perhaps you were as intelligent—and, of course, more studious—than he was, but he had street smarts. He was a precocious adolescent. He already knew how to drive and smoke, and, according to him, he wasn't a virgin anymore. While all of us were sitting way up in the highest tree on their property, Uriarte told intricate stories to you and Correa and Arce, who had also been invited to Cuernavaca. He described the undergarments of the woman with whom he had gone to bed. As you listened to the minute description of how— little by little, one by one—she had started to remove her clothes, you suddenly became aroused! And, making it even more exciting, at the same time that Uriarte was expanding the end of the story, your crotch was also expanding, much the same way it did when you thought about the three acorns covering Ana Bertha Lepe's near-naked body. As a result, you were unable to sit comfortably on the highest branches of the largest tree at Uriarte's house. Since his birthday coincided with Independence Day, school was closed. The four of you, including some younger cousins, had been left alone at Uriarte's. Having spent the weekend in Cuernavaca for his birthday, his parents had already returned to Mexico City and wouldn't be back to get all of you until Tuesday night. As soon as you said good-bye to them that Sunday afternoon, smiling profusely and then watching the black Oldsmobile disappear down the road, the four of you suddenly felt perversely free. Uriarte immediately exercised his authority as host and demanded money from everyone in order to buy some Bacardi. There was going to be a party that night with just the four of you and four girls, one for each. It seemed like it was a holdup, having to quickly empty your pockets and come up with enough money to buy three bottles of rum and Cokes. Then you started to fix up the living room, putting the bottles, Cokes, ice, and four tall glasses, each with a different color and number, on the coffee table. Yours was number seven, dark blue. After forty years, how can you still remember that, Juan Manuel! You were excited, perhaps not so much about the impending drinking spree or the possibility of having sex as for the pleasure you felt upon defying family rules and venturing into prohibited territory: don't ever drink, son, remember what happened to your uncle Severino, your father's brother, who lost everything—fortune, fame, and family—because of alcohol, so don't ever drink, be careful, it runs in the family. At the time, you wanted to be bold, act like an adult, and show everyone that you had been around the block. That was when, as if you were an old pro at it, you inhaled for the first time and found yourself inebriated even before you had taken your first drink. Uriarte's first round was too strong. He scoffed at Arce, who was uneasy about the whole thing. You could tell that his conscience was weighing heavily on him. Making sure you didn't become a target of mockery, you quickly chimed in with "Cheers," clinking your glass with the others—the dark blue seven with the red three, the pale-blue six, and the green two. Now, many years later, you can still see those numbers, hear the clinking crystal, and the jangle of ice cubes, as if that were the moment when the numbers were added up and averaged. Uriarte put on a stack of records that played continuously—Ray Conniff, Sonora Mancera, Agustín Lara's "La hora íntima" for the girls— Benny Moré, Los Panchos, and Los Churumbeles from Spain . . . Ugh! Your initial glee turned to euphoria. Unable to quench your thirst, you drank continuously. Nearing fifteen years of age, that night you made up for what you had not consumed until that point in your life. You drank everything you had been told not to drink, everything that your Uncle Severino had consumed in a lifetime, and every last drop of alcohol that runs in the family. Your body was soaking up that rum, and while you waited for the girls who never came, of course, you continued to knock back glass after glass. Your behavior became insane. Today, Juan Manuel, you can't remember with much clarity what happened that night. Perhaps you wanted to forget it all the next day, especially when you had to confront a hangover and disgrace for the first time in your life. Anyway, do you remember that sudden burst of energy and wanting to go for a swim? All of you jumped into the pool to see who could swim the most laps. You challenged Arce, Correa, and Uriarte, who were as drunk as you were. Where did this ability to swim come from, Juan Manuel? You had never done anything more than paddle around in the water, trying to stay afloat. Having never played sports, you preferred intellectual pursuits to physical activities. Fortunately, Uriarte's cousin Gus got wind of your challenge, Juan Manuel, and rounded up his brothers to stop you guys from ending up in serious trouble. All of you might have drowned. Uriarte's cousins tied you and your friends up to stop you from jumping into the pool while you were drunk, especially you, Juan Manuel, who didn't know how to swim. They tied your wrists together first, then your ankles, and just to make sure, they put a noose around your neck, as if you were a dog, tied the other end to the bathroom doorknob, and locked the door behind them. Nevertheless, you kept yelling and daring everyone to jump into the pool. Despite your deplorable condition, you were feeling pretty damn good. You actually thrived on being the center of attention, pampered, creating fear, causing worry, and threatening Uriarte's cousins with your antics. They were so young, yet so well behaved. You had heard that you can get rid of a hangover by putting ice cubes on your testicles. After all these years, you can still feel the burning cold. After that experiment, you fell asleep next to the toilet. You woke up heaving, and that's when you began feeling like shit. That was the first time you felt the onslaught of a hangover that would repeat itself so many more times in your life, similar to the way you feel this morning, forty years later, victimized at midday, despite the restorative beers and your resignation. You promised yourself: never again. Feeling remorse the next morning, your head had become overly sensitive to even the smallest noise and was ready to explode like a hand grenade. You were musing with your friends over the mayhem of the previous night when you heard the sound of an approaching car. What's going on? Are they coming back early? Could it be Tuesday already? No, man, are you crazy? It's only Monday. It was Uriarte's mother. She had returned alone. She looked out of sorts, nervous. She acted like she didn't want to enter the house. You were expecting a reprimand, but she didn't seem to notice anything wrong, not even the mess—empty bottles, dirty glasses, overflowing ashtrays, sticky floors, the smell of vomit. Without any explanation, she said in a low voice that she had come to get you, Barrientos, only you. It was urgent that she take you back to Mexico City. Don't worry, she would explain everything on the way back. But, of course, you got worried. What could have happened? Your mother and sister came to mind. Gathering up your things, you put them in your suitcase. You tried to look serious and mature when you said good-bye to your friends. They, too, were frightened and pale, if not from the pending tragedy, then from the effects of the hangovers. You got into the front seat next to Mrs. Uriarte. She was still nervous and unable to give you any explanation as to why she had gone to pick you up. Scared, you didn't want to ask her either. You didn't want to know anything. It wasn't just the feeling of impending doom that upset you, it was also the way you were feeling. You even thought that anything, no matter how tragic, had to be less painful than your hangover. Why get bad news just when you're in no shape to receive it? How can you take any bad news when you can't even stand the sun hitting the windshield or the sound of the car motor? Why was Mrs. Uriarte driving so slowly? Why did she take so long to shift gears? It was hard to contain your nausea, but even if you had had to tell her to stop so you could get out and throw up, she'd never have suspected that the cause was drinking; instead, she would have thought that it was because of the bad news that she was still unable to give you. Now you were sure it had to be bad news. If it weren't bad news, she wouldn't have driven all the way back to Cuernavaca to get you. The trip back seemed interminable. When she finally turned onto your street, Mrs. Uriarte was unable to park the car. As if there were a wedding going on next door, the street was packed with cars. Halfway up the block, she gave you a hug and began to cry, but she still didn't say a word. She just couldn't say anything. Walking to the front door, you were confused, nervous, and feeling sick. You didn't have to ring the doorbell, because your entire family was there to meet you, including distant aunts and uncles—all dressed in black—whom you never saw except on holidays. They all hugged you, pinched your cheek as if you were still a little boy, and said "poor thing" over and over. You were wondering what was going on here when you heard a low murmuring. Prayers. Once inside the house, you saw it in the middle of the living room, surrounded by white flowers and women in mourning—the casket. Juan Manuel is back, said Ángel, your half-brother. You never saw him much, because he didn't live in Mexico City. Besides, he was much older than you. And there were no tears behind those dark glasses. When your mother appeared, she hugged you like never before, kissed you on the forehead, and ran her fingers through your hair. What's happened? you asked her with anguish. You mean Mrs. Uriarte didn't tell you? Then you imagined that you were the dead person, Juan Manuel. These ladies were crying over your death, which had taken place in Cuernavaca the night before. Maybe you had drowned in the swimming pool at Uriarte's house, Juan Manuel. You were purple, stiff, and cold.

Even today, you can still hear those sounds. Standing at the entrance amid that communal silence surrounded by cypress trees, Ángel wouldn't let you descend into the family crypt. But then you hear the sound of the shovel stirring the cement, sand, and water, until it finally thickens into a small mound. Next, you hear the crumbling cement blocks being dragged across the marble floor, as if prisoners were dragging chains. Then comes the sound of the trowel layering the cement between the blocks. When the niche for the casket is finally bricked in, leaving no crack through which his last breath can escape, the mason hurls the last bit of cement, as if he were spitting, against the new wall. Then he smoothes it out, ready to receive the gravestone with your father's name on it, including (in parentheses) his birth date and the year of his death.

As if condemned to life in prison, he has been trapped and jailed, and he will never be able to escape.

The back of his head. You remember him with his back to you, sitting at his desk facing the wall, as if he were being punished. You remember him wearing his blue flannel robe, the worn-out slippers, and the white beard, always three days old. You remember him doing absolutely nothing, frittering away his retirement and losing his memory. He was living in a past that always produced a spark in his sad eyes, and when it disappeared, all that was left was a nostalgic smile on his lips. Every day, he would read the newspaper ever so meticulously, from beginning to end. In addition, he would cross out the articles that he had already read, because by then his memory was like a sieve. What difference did it make, you asked yourself once, if he had already forgotten them? He could easily reread them as if he had never read them. That wouldn't be so bad, because the entire exercise was solely to kill time anyway, that is, to make time pass, as if he were a permanent insomniac, whose dreams were never interrupted except for the daydreaming that stemmed from staring at the bare walls of his study. Nevertheless, it was a certain modesty that stimulated him to cross out the newspaper articles in order to conceal his obvious amnesia. What else do you remember about him? His monkish austerity. His inaudible voice. His penetrating eyes, which were fixed on the horizon, despite the walls of his study. His deafness, despite the almost always turned off hearing aid wrapped around his ear. His knees, when once upon a time—you can barely remember it among your earliest memories—you played horsey.

How could I talk to you, Papa, if you always had your back to me while you stared at the horizon through the wall? Why try to talk to you, if you were deaf and didn't remember anything, neither the newspaper articles nor me? You left me without saying good-bye. I would like to talk to you, and I want you to listen to me, to recognize me, to help me through the throbbing of this goddamn hangover. But you don't hear me, you can't hear me, because you're deaf and you've lost your memory. You've turned your back on me.

• • • • •

Shrouded by the pious but inharmonious voices of the choir wafting upwards, Juan Manuel abandoned the San Francisco cloister, only to be engulfed by the deafening hue and cry of the twentieth century outside.

CHAPTER 3

A FEW BLOCKS later, Juan Manuel Barrientos came upon another local bar, but this one was straight out of the Porfirio Díaz era, with all of its nineteenth-century French trappings, which had been transformed into some form of virile crudeness, in much the same way that Porfirio himself, despite his knowledge of artillery, missed the spittoons in the luxurious salons at Chapultepec Castle and hit the Persian rugs.

Whenever one of these bars had a sign hanging next to the door-jamb that prohibited women, as well as minors and people in uniform, you could pretty well expect to find sawdust spread all over the floor inside that functioned to absorb just about any and every kind of damp and humid excretion. Depending on the day of the week, you could order the "drink of the day" and different kinds of appetizers. Roasted chickens were raffled off. Electric shocks were available to slow down getting drunk or to determine okay you pussies, who's more macho. And for the guy returning home late to an angry wife, there were all kinds of safe-conducts—records by Los Panchos, real orchids in cellophane packages, or sexual-potency enhancers.

Its name was La Ópera, and like other similar places, no table-cloths were used, which made for moving dominoes around more easily. And the elegance of yesteryear—stuffed velvet armchairs, rococo decorations, hand-carved moldings, brocaded silk tapestries, ornate candelabras, paintings of the French countryside, and the stately wooden bar that had come from the old Café Colón—stood out against the vulgarity of the drunks who would show up around noon and for the rest of the day drink and play dominoes while listening to musicians who went from bar to bar playing their most sentimental songs. Before women were allowed, La Ópera had a special room in the back for wives who, not unlike those Adelitas following their men into battle during the Mexican Revolution, would enter from Filomeno Mata Street and wait patiently while their men got drunk.

After women were no longer prohibited from frequenting those bars, changes did take place, and who knows if it was for better or worse. True, now you could certainly enjoy the pleasure of female companionship in those places that had been fiercely masculine, have a drink, talk, confess, and even share the feeling of euphoria with a loved or desired woman, or both. Lost is the possibility of talking about those women without the distraction, the formality, or the inhibitions that their very presence usually imposed. In those places, feelings and emotions radiated straight from the heart, especially when it was about women and their beauty, grace, sophistication, or other things, like hope, desire, jealousy, resentment, and disillusionment. They're the topics that passionate love eternally provoked in men. Still, women also triggered feelings of sorrow, pride at having conquered, pain, desperation, anger, violence—all of which, according to the relationship or affair, were usually followed by audible sighs, laughter, obscene smirks, tears, sniveling, and always booze . . . and lots of it, too. Isn't that right, buddy? To celebrate, to remember, to forget, or to say fuck this, goddam bitches, the whores. Right, buddy? Nowadays, however, with the possibility of having a woman sit right there next to you, invariably words went unsaid, and those bars became much more restrained.

White tablecloths smothered the tapping of the dominoes, the loud laughter and swearing had become muted, arguments died on the vine, and it even smelled nicer inside. Somehow, the atmosphere was subdued and, undoubtedly, more cerebral.

Since Juan Manuel had no intention of eating anything, at least not yet anyway, and given that he was by himself, he didn't sit down at any of the tables reserved for groups of friends in that saloon with velvet chairs that seemed more appropriate for the dining car of a presidential train than a restaurant. Instead, he took a seat at the bar, where his image was reflected in the mirror in front of him, along with rows of liquor bottles, the oak columns sustaining the back of the bar, and the yellowish gold, grease-stained wooden scrolling that framed it all.

Barrientos, you find true pleasure in sitting at the bar with that strange collection of bottles, the different shapes and sizes of glassware from shot glasses to beer mugs, and that mirror, that is to say, your conscience when you drink alone or, more likely, with yourself, who is as well the conversant that lets you look indirectly at other strangers sitting at the bar and carry on a conversation with them without having to look at them, that is to say, without having to expose yourself to their intrusions. How many hours of your life have you spent sitting in front of mirrors at bars, alternating one foot or the other on the barstool rung, staring at your reflection, rebuffing it at times, and at other times, doting on it with tenderness? Tell me, how many hours has it been? If you dared to add them up, they would become days, weeks, months, and even years.

It doesn't take much to convince Jimena and Fernando that you're not breaking the rules of the game that consists of one drink per bar, just because you're ordering a beer with a shot of tequila. You explain—well, you're always explaining things—that, in addition to being the drink of moderation, beer is simply a chaser for the tequila, because one of its ingredients, yeast, serves as a protective layer to the stomach lining. As a result, when you rigorously knock back a shot of tequila, an act sustained by the oldest ritual in Mexico, the liquor splashes on top of a foamy cushion that protects our insides from irritation and acidity. And judging from the academic vocabulary that you usually use for explaining even the most mundane topics, your students would listen to you attentively—well, they would've listened to you had they been here today—similar to the way they took notes and listened to you lecture about Sor Juana's "First Dream" or baroque pilasters.

However, at the bar they served you three drinks—a mug of beer, a shot of tequila, and a sangrita chaser.

You're alone, Juan Manuel, so you can knock back three or four drinks, one right after the other, which cures hangovers once and for all. And you can do it without having to talk to anyone around you. But you must restrain yourself and hold back as much as possible, because you still have several more stops to make.

Right off the bat, you reject the sangrita and take a long sip of beer, which is tequila's best friend. Satisfying your thirst, the beer allows the tequila to concentrate on its own energy, strength, and nuances. Just imagine trying to quench your thirst with tequila. Well, you'd be dead by now, Juan Manuel, because your thirst is insatiable, boundless. You take a second swig of beer and ponder the tiny double ring of pearls that forms on the surface of the tequila. Judiciously, you sprinkle salt on a slice of lime. The you pick up the shot of tequila, raise it in a toast that the mirror behind the rows of vodka and gin bottles reflects back at you in a friendly way, and down it in one gulp, like yesterday at Casa Pedro, and like every day, as always, down the hatch, burning all the way down. Jesus! Tequila isn't to be savored. It's supposed to go straight down, no swishing it around in your mouth, because the good feeling it produces comes afterward, when you exhale, when its vapors resurface from below, from your stomach, in your breath. It's then, and not before, when the lime with a dash of salt blends sharply with the tequila, because in reality you're supposed to inhale tequila in the same way you inhale smoke from a cigarette. Tequila is a drink that you inhale. After quivering for a moment, you immediately feel a rush, a loss of body, and then everything returns to normal. And there's nothing like tequila to cure a hangover. It puts your stomach in order, reconnects all of the bones in your body, and brings light to your dark thoughts and the blindness of your mind. It also prepares you for the next round. Here's your theory: the first shot of tequila rescues you from lethargy; the second shot produces happiness and euphoria; and the third creates a feeling of serenity. However, the fourth shot can be dangerous. It might incite depression. Anything after that, you lose. One should never drink more than three shots of tequila.

Sometimes they make you apathetic, but you do care about them just the same, especially when they're not with you. And you really wish they were with you now, so that you could take them back to your old stomping grounds, always amid a display of budding wisdom. They try so hard to please you, to voice mature opinions, and to be a part of what's going on! Antonio was responsible for organizing the excursion. Why didn't he show up? Why didn't he answer your phone calls? It's so strange! Couldn't he have at least let you know that he wasn't coming? You know that he respects you, even though he's seen you lose it more than once. Many times he's had to take you home after you got drunk! More than your disciple, more than your teaching assistant, Antonio is your personal aide. Many times over you have sorely disappointed him. And someday his disappointment will be irreversible. Oh, Juan Manuel, you act like life will always save you from having to ask for his help. Feeling both admiration and scorn, Antonio must be confused about his relationship with you. Even though he might believe that he still needs your guidance before breaking away, it's possible that with your retirement he feels free from your tutelage after so many years. Oh, don't be so arrogant: you're more dependent upon him than he is upon you. What's more, he's probably gone from your life forever. Maybe that's why he's not here today. There has to be a reason why he didn't answer your calls. Is it possible that you said something to upset him yesterday? You don't remember anything. You've got such a bad memory. And what about Fernando? Of course, it was Fernando who suggested that they meet downtown. It's strange that he hasn't shown up either! He's so polite, so well-mannered. You detected in him the same literary sensitivity that you once had, which now only triggers feelings of nostalgia. It was that same sensitivity that lured him to your course on the baroque in the first place, which ended up requiring you to teach it in terms of an explanation of your own contradictions and hand wringing. He's intelligent and possesses a clarity of vision that has grown over time, or at least remained constant, all of which makes him an exceptional person. He's knowledgeable, his curiosity is unswerving, and he's interested in everything. It would have been great if he had come along. With him at your side, the tour you're about to undertake, that is, the one that you've already initiated, would've been easier for you. Or maybe harder. And why hasn't Jimena shown up? She seemed so excited about going on a downtown tour. And her presence would have stimulated you. She's more intelligent than Fernando. She's got it all together. And how you miss her gestures, her low voice, her healthy teeth! Now that these bars allow women, she could be here next to you. But even if she were here, you could only pine for her, imagine her, desire her. More than someone who is baroque in nature, you're a simple romantic son of a bitch!

Even though you can't possess her, you want to occupy a space in her heart, touch her intimately, love her, and be loved. But somehow you come to understand that, between being conceited and guilty, you'd probably ruin her without realizing that the one who would be destroyed would be you, Juan Manuel. Sooner or later, Jimena would reject the admiration that she now professes for you. She would become disgusted with the dictatorial erudition and whims that you've been creating throughout your academic life. In short, subjected to the humiliation of her beauty and youth, you're the one who would be destroyed, not her.

You take another sip of beer.

She showed up at your office one day without an appointment. She knocked on your door in a flirtatious way that at the time you didn't pick up on. Without taking your eyes off of the computer screen, where a phrase was fighting intrepidly to jettison an inadmissible gerund, you said come in. She entered your small academic space with the poise of a prima ballerina who was going on stage. And there she stood, her hand still on the doorknob, until you finally abandoned your quandary over the phrase and looked up at her. Her tight pants, her long, flowing hair, and her smile that was bigger than your cubicle, the building, or the whole university, immediately aroused you. I'm Jimena, she said. Nothing more. Mesmerized, you somehow managed to invite her into your musty workplace, which was overflowing with books, magazines, and photographs. You removed a pile of papers from the only other chair, and she sat down directly in front of you, touching your knees with hers. She hadn't been able to register for your class, she said, with that low, raspy voice, whose first words immediately seduced you. I'm Jimena, and I was hoping to sit in on your seminar. That's what she was after: to get into your class with your disciples. Without questioning her academic background, you instantly said yes. You could have imposed certain conditions, recommended particular readings, provided a bibliography for the course, but nothing came to mind except to approve her request, while you, like a babbling idiot, were completely taken by her beauty. It was your birthday that day. Antonio had given you a tie. What else could Antonio have given you if it weren't this nondescript tie that you would never wear? And the telltale birthday tie with intersecting blue and gold diagonal stripes stood out next to the gift box on top of your desk. It's your birthday, huh? she asked. Yes, you admitted, with a certain asinine fear that the next question would be how old you were, which would have put a lot of distance between you and this radiant beauty sitting in your office, as if one couldn't tell by your graying temples, wrinkled face, and flaccid skin. Fortunately, she didn't ask any more questions, and as if you had always known her, and despite the difference in your ages, your backgrounds, and your pasts, you did have a lot in common: you were accomplices in creating humor. And you said straight up, Yep, it's my birthday, so how about a hug? She gave you one of those generous smiles, stood up from the uncomfortable chair that you had offered her, and gave you one of those unforgettable hugs. You could have kissed her and made love to her right there on top of your books and magazines. It would have been your birthday present. It was as if someone had sent her to you like an after-dinner drink from a friend sitting at a nearby table in a restaurant; or better yet, she had appeared in your office to help you smother the indifference that you were feeling from the brutal pain inflicted upon you by the other one, the one who you were unable to assimilate into your life. It was a smile that could easily turn to sadness, from desire to bereavement. And in order to hold on to that one, you let this one go that morning. She left the same way she had come—like the Angel of the Annunciation.

Once and for all, you're ready to take the second shot of tequila of the day—the one that produces happiness and euphoria, according to your theoretical disquisitions. Impulsively, you're about to order another one, which will send straight to hell the rules of the game that you yourself imposed on your students. So, if they haven't shown up yet, why follow the rules? They've left you high and dry. Who cares if you've broken the rules since leaving Salón La Luz? Besides, Juan Manuel, here a shot of tequila and a beer add up to two drinks. Don't be such a jerk. You contain yourself. Don't order anything else, just the check. You finished the beer that in practice didn't produce any of that protection about which you delivered a lecture earlier. The acidity forces you to chew a Maalox tablet. You pay the bill and leave.

· · · · ·

You could have continued along Cinco de Mayo Street, but you chose Filomeno Mata, on the side of the old School of Mining, in order to walk down Tacuba toward the Zócalo, the main plaza and center of Mexico City. Anyway, that was the plan, even though the true center is hidden in the bowels of the earth and has multiplied itself infinitely through a verse of the Mexican national anthem: "Y retiemble en sus centros la tierra," meaning "And let the earth tremble at its centers." Here, it was as if the earth had several centers, that is, as if the center—the epicenter—equally distant from other centers, configuring the circumference, and giving the center precisely its condition of centeredness, according to its definition, was not just one but many centers. It wasn't a rhetorical figure, like the one that multiplies the essence of the nation or its destiny in order to make it sound more sonorous or emphatic—the *destinies* of the nation, the *essences* of the homeland. No. The idea of several *centers* was something else. Explaining the phenomenon to Jimena and Fernando in that unbearable professional tone, you say that to you the anthem's original version says "*antros*" instead of "*centros*," that is, caverns instead of centers. Haphazardly, the songwriter González Bocanegra must have transcribed some of the letters in such a way that they were interpreted differently, and since then, have become a part of the official record and the public domain. As a result, "And let the earth tremble at its centers" should have been "And let the earth tremble in its caverns," because back then "*antros*" didn't have the connotation that it has today, that is, dingy, disreputable bars or dives, like you would have wanted it to mean, but only the innermost recesses or centers, that is, caverns, caves, or grottos. "And let the earth tremble in its caverns" meant just that, its caves and grottos. So, why not say, "And let the earth tremble from within?" That doesn't sound so bad, does it? The verse would be longer and more fitting for the rhythm of a national anthem, you exclaim while gesticulating wildly. This is crazy! We've had to add syllables to every verse forever and ever in order to make them fit the music: [*heaven*] *ha-has given you a soldier in every son*. Do you see what I mean? *Mexicans, at the cry of wa-war, / prepare the steel and the ste-eed / And may the earth shake at its co-ore / to the resounding roar of the-e cannon*. Like any other anthem, ours is a fighting, warlike, violent hymn, but we've had to stutter, adding syllables, to make it work.

Bolstered by the strange pleasure he got from the combination of tequila and philology—centers, caverns, and dingy bars—Juan Manuel Barrientos walked to the Tolsá Plaza, so secret yet so mag-

nificent. He commented on the architectural style of the Department of Natural Resources and the sculpture of the horse, "Caballito," by an architect from Valencia. Using his umbrella, he pointed
out the protruding chest of the animal while explaining to Jimena
and Fernando how in his youth he would hurry from the Zócalo to
the inner patio of the old university, which long ago disappeared,
except for the stone entryway that was inherited by San Pablo College and the doors that went to the University Club. From there,
he would continue along the Bucarelli Promenade at the beginning
of Juárez Avenue, exactly where you met him, Jimena, don't tell me
you don't remember, you're so young, Heavens alive! How humili-
atingly young you are, until he got to this intimate little plaza in
front of Natural Resources that was constructed by Tolsá himself.
However, he wasn't as interested in that plaza as he was with the
center of the city, so he started out along Tacuba, heading toward
the Zócalo, the very center, where, if it trembles, the earth will
tremble spasmodically from the sonorous roar of a ca-ca-cannon.

He walked past an old colonial-style mansion—now a run-of-
the-mill billiards hall and gymnasium—that once belonged to the
family of Doña Carmelita Romero Rubio, the wife of Porfirio Díaz.
At noon on Fridays, you could hear the breaking of billiard balls,
the vociferous betting, and loud insults; in the gym, young men of
a proletarian nature dreamed of becoming bodybuilders like the
ones on the posters on the walls as they lifted enormous weights in
front of unforgiving mirrors. He was unable to contain his rarefied
preference for the old center of the city, which in some obscene way
included its misery, folly, and universal deterioration. In response,
he scurried down a narrow side street replete with street vendors
selling trinkets and candy in order to show his students the vestibule of that French palace, now totally concealed from view. To the
right, there was a majestic marble staircase with a broken banister
to which they had added a grotesque landing midway up in order
to provide an entrance to a dental clinic. He went up the stairs to
the first landing. He turned and looked upward, which is what his
students would have done, and pointed with his umbrella at the

marvelous dome above, which was supported by bronze caryatids. At some point in the past, the dome contained a stained-glass skylight that corresponded to the beauty of the surrounding architecture. Much of the glass was now broken, and like bad trapeze artists, pieces had fallen into a net below that, in addition to catching the translucent, multicolored remnants, functioned as a way to trap bats inhabiting the dome, even though it was impossible to keep in check the excrement and other filth that dripped onto the walls and the Carrara marble staircase. Having successfully met the challenge to impress his students with a presentation of such a spectacle, which was both magnificent and pitiful at the same time, he went back outside and crossed the street in order to give Jimena and Fernando a better view of the small palace. It had been a splendid building made of marble balconies and garrets, *comme il faut*, although now it had been degraded by grime, missing window panes, scroungers and their stalls, and the signs for the billiard hall, the gym, and a camera shop, where you could get black and white hand-colored portraits. Fernando, you mean you've never seen this building before? We continued walking down the street, staring straight ahead without looking up, perhaps to avoid the dull gray sky, which seemed so sticky. In order to visualize the architecture, Jimena, you must look above the store windows and in your mind eliminate the commercial signs, electric lines, and excrement.

He kept walking toward the Zócalo, but once he got to Motolinía, instead of going down Tacuba, as he had proposed, he turned back toward Cinco de Mayo. If it had been his intention to go to the Zócalo by way of a more decent street like Tacuba, why take that street? Well, you're hungry now and you just had this crazy idea, totally against your will, to head toward Bar Alfonso. Motolinía was packed with street vendors with their stalls selling polyethylene, pornographic videos, cheap watches, contraband, and U.S. military toys, the boxes for which were piled up like garbage in the streets. It could have been either Christmas or a war zone.

It wasn't easy making his way down the street through the conglomeration of aggressive vendors that engulfed him in a sea of sweat and loud hawking of goods. Walking toward Bar Alfonso, he stepped on the pit of a mango, which only biologists call a "seed." He slipped, lost his balance, and fell to his knees on the sidewalk. Feeling stupid amid the turmoil around him, you immediately get up so as not to provoke the laughter that falling down like that tends to provoke.

It was nothing, you say quickly before any vendors rush to your aid. It was nothing, you repeat, brushing the dirt from the sleeves of your tweed jacket, wiping off your pants, and simultaneously running your fingers through your hair like a comb.

CHAPTER 4

WITH TWO large mirrors facing each other, the inside of Dar Alfonso seemed to extend forever.

The tables lining the walls were all taken. Providing protection from people staring from nearby tables, they're always the preferred spots in just about any restaurant, not to mention that they offer the best places to watch people without being noticed yourself. Luckily, there was a table near the window that looked out on one side of the Paris Building, without having to look farther down the street at the green river of vendor stalls. The maître d' assigned one of the more seasoned waiters to his table. Juan Manuel gave a sigh of relief. Even though he was feeling a bit better than earlier in the day, his senses were still at risk. The bright light hurt his eyes, and the rattling of plates and silverware, seemingly tossed about with that Hispanic brusqueness and without wall hangings or curtains to soften the din, had left him panicky. In addition, the noisy conversation and laughter at a nearby table was irritating him. A restaurant of this category is usually quieter.

He didn't know why he was there. Of course, he had always liked the place. It was charming, refined but austere, and the food and drink were good, too. Nevertheless, he would have preferred that his tour take him to another restaurant, where he could resume the process of curing his hangover with a bowl of spicy shrimp soup and where his loneliness would be less obvious. He detested having to dine alone, especially if he happened to be in a comfortable, elegant restaurant. Seemingly, the ambience was being wasted without someone in your company. It's true that he could live alone and eat breakfast alone; in addition, he needed his solitude for reading, writing, working, and thinking, but not for eating out. How can you discuss the flavor of the fish, the taste of the meat, or the virtues of the wine? How can you toast someone's health alone? Nevertheless, he still would have preferred not to eat right then, but if you were somehow violating your disposition to eat, and to eat well, you would've been a goner a long time ago, Juan Manuel. Now, he was sitting at that table with a cloth napkin and wine and crystal surrounding him, which he had imposed upon himself, in order not to have to endure the humility that loneliness could invoke in him. He wasn't there because he wanted to be there, but now that you are, you should have every right to eat well and to see if you can clear out those cobwebs of depression.

Distinguished, beautiful, and now in the prime of her life, a woman was reflected in the mirror. She had put up her hair in a bun that gracefully—with pride—displayed her gray hair. She was talking with another woman, and a man, most likely the other woman's husband, sat distractedly next to her.

Even before the waiter could ask him what he wanted to drink, he hastily ordered a beer and a shot of white Herradura tequila— the second of the day, and it was already nearing three o'clock in the afternoon. He wanted it served in a large shot glass instead of a cognac snifter. Despite his insatiability, he still maintained a preference for doing things a certain way, which had become an obsession in his older years. No matter how desperate he was, he would never drink a beer directly from the bottle, much less a can or plastic cup.

The pleasure of drinking that he meticulously conserved, despite being a compulsive drinker, was simply his modus operandi and had become a part of the ceremony. Tequila must be served to the brim in a "caballito," a special shot glass just for tequila, even though with each successive drink the possibility of spilling it became more apparent. Beer must be consumed in a crystal glass or transparent mug, just so long as it wasn't too thick, so as not to blur the golden luminosity of that effervescent, bubbly liquid. During the daytime at least, he could defend his obsessions against commonplace and indiscriminate ways of drinking alcohol. He knew how to drink, that is, he knew good brands of liquor, and he knew how to drink them. He also ate well, but his alcohol consumption had relegated his appetite to a lesser need. And he really enjoyed reading restaurant menus, as if they were a literary genre unto their own. Often he was more stimulated by sheer poetic pleasure than gastronomic gratification. Some dishes sounded better than they actually were: lobster with asparagus; steamed cod with sweet basil over puréed Swiss chard; white fish macerated in mescal; sweetbreads in red pepper sauce; crème brûlée; guanábana sorbet. What great words! *Sweet basil. Lobster. Sea bass. Crème brûlée. Guanábana.*

He didn't want to use the restroom just yet. The urge to urinate can be put off for a while, but when you go for the first time, there's no way of stopping from going again after that. Perhaps you should have your prostate checked. And after that the need to go becomes more frequent and urgent. In reality, that moment had just arrived. While your drink was being brought to you, you went to release three beers, gushing somewhere between your stomach and your bladder.

The stream was accurate, abundant, and sonorous. He also took a moment to brush off some dirt remaining from his fall, because he thought he might look even more ridiculous than he already did. And he washed the same hands upon which he had fallen. He splashed water on his face. When he looked into the mirror, he saw a glint of youthful radiance. Then he returned to his table, ready to consume his tequila and beer.

You take a sip of beer. Although somewhat unsteady, you still raise the shot glass of tequila with resolute protocol. You haven't lost that penchant for ceremony, even when you drink alone. You feel obliged to drink a toast to yourself or to someone's absence. And, now, in one of those rare moments of fate that you fail to understand, your raised shot glass brimming with tequila coincides in the mirror with a similar gesture from the gray-haired lady, who all the while is giving you a generous smile. And two shot glasses became enamored. How marvelous!

Immediately, your body undergoes a retrospective transformation. Automatically, your stomach shrinks and you suck in your stomach. Without being able to control it, your double chin tightens, while your thorax expands and all of your vertebrae fall into place. Sitting erect, you quickly knock back the shot without even glancing away from the mirror, impervious and direct, that reflects the warmth of her mouth and a splendid set of teeth. You can easily succumb to the beauty of a female set of teeth and even find pleasure in their minor imperfections, such as the tiny space between the two front teeth that the Archpriest of Hita talked about—don't you remember, Dr. Academic?—when discussing the beauty of the ideal woman. Later, unable to comprehend the Islamic sensuality that was inherent in that visible space, Spanish scribes closed the gap by changing its meaning.

When dining in a restaurant of this caliber, he knew full well that it was customary to order a bottle of wine. So, he skipped the lime, because it anesthetizes the taste buds and prevents you from savoring wine in all its fullness. Nevertheless, you had already sucked on a slice of lime in La Ópera, not to mention the effects that tequila has on your taste buds. It is definitely an aperitif, of course, but if you're going to combine it with wine, then tequila should be an after-dinner cordial.

Before ordering, he requested another shot of tequila—the one that activates serenity and peace. He enjoyed reading the menu and ordered some stock dishes, such as Serrano ham for an entrée; next, given that it was warm outside, he ordered gazpacho; and for the main dish, suckling pig. Perfect!

Nevertheless, in order to cure his hangover he would have preferred a seafood soup, euphemistically called "Return to Life," that Luis made at the Mixcoac market and that consisted of oysters, shrimp, herbs, avocado, and a spicy hot habanero pepper sauce that always brought tears to your eyes. But the beers and shots of tequila had put him on solid ground. He was feeling a little better now. At least he wasn't nauseous anymore, and he even felt a little hungry. Besides, he was in a Spanish restaurant, and it was time to enjoy one of those infanticides upon which the laurels of Spanish cuisine rest—baby goat, lamb, or roast suckling pig.

It wasn't about eating, but rather about going from bar to bar as they—the professor and his disciples—had agreed upon yesterday in Casa Pedro. No such luck. His trajectory, a bad one at that, had led him to a restaurant and a bottle of wine. Since that kind of food can only be consumed with red wine, independently of his established rules, he ordered a bottle. No one should ever order just half a bottle, even if you're alone, because you inexorably end up ordering two half bottles. Ribera del Duero. Pesquera. Wine wasn't the best medicine for curing a hangover, but what the hell . . . one thing for sure, he was feeling better. And suckling pig without wine?

Hearing the gray-haired woman laugh, you turn to look, but simultaneously she does the same thing. Is she looking at you? And there's that full set of teeth. What a candid mouth! Such sparkling eyes! Once again, you raise your refilled shot glass, toast each other, and then you vigorously knock back the tequila. You're losing weight. The tequila reabsorbs the fat that has accumulated in your body, and suddenly your muscles become taut. Despite the daily sixteen minutes that you spend on the stationary bicycle, the flaccid protrusion of your expanding waist and the colorless flab that joins your arms to your defeated pectorals are now suppressed by the straight lines of youthful virility.

The ham, when carefully cut into thin slices with a knife, as it should be, curls up naturally. And you relive your favorite nightmare: You have a piece of Serrano ham in front of you, and you know that one part of it is poisoned. You don't know which part, but if you take the wrong bite, you'll fall dead on the spot. You cut the ham ever so thinly. You eat it. It tastes marvelous. Absolutely wonderful. You're happy that you didn't eat the poisoned part. You're saved, but you can't stop yourself from cutting another slice. And another. And another. And another.

They ask you to taste the wine. You hold the glass up against the light. It's an impressively clear and glossy dark red wine. Your eyes brighten, and the shininess that was barely visible when you went to the bathroom now expands toward your iris and out to the whites of your eyes. Next, you sniff it. Its intense primary aroma inflates your nostrils. Finally, you take a sip. Great range, dry, and full-bodied, you state with a revived palate for the gray-haired lady, who looks at herself in the mirror exactly where you're reflected as well.

Although the gazpacho doesn't have the healing qualities of that seafood soup, it still revives you. Suddenly, you feel younger. There's something childlike, even magical, about this painter's palette of jovial colors that combines the red soup with green peppers, the tearful whiteness of the onions, the light green cucumbers, and the earthy gold croutons.

The wine swathes your mouth, tongue, palate, and throat. It reaches your nostrils, and from inside the aroma overtakes you. And you see it from the inside, too, like a dark tide that submerges a coral reef—your teeth. You hold it in your mouth until your stomach and its conduits begin to clamor for it.

There's no denying it—she's looking at you in the mirror. If your students had been here, you would've initiated a conversation in which you'd be the centerpiece, the actor, gesturing excessively. Actually, you're more interested in form than content. You want to demonstrate to her that you're capable of mesmerizing Jimena and Fernando, as if by extension, you would capture her attention as well. Unable to hear your words, she can only perceive the meaning of your slight murmuring. Each time she sees you in the mirror, you glance back at her. And each time you look at her you feel younger and younger. The puffiness of your face magically shrinks away, that is, the swelling—caused by the alcohol—between your eyebrows and your eyes that has hidden your eyelids, your flaccid cheeks, and the broken blood vessels in your nose.

The waiter brings out your plate of roast suckling pig—part of the front leg and a corresponding piece of the lower ribs.

How old were you back then, Juanma, as they called you? Six? Maybe seven years old? It must have been during the Christmas holidays, between first and second grades, when the school year corresponded to the calendar year. Classes began in February and ended in November, so that the vacation period was dedicated mostly to celebrating Christmas, from the Posadas—those family and neighborhood festivities from December 16 to 24, to the day when the Three Wise Men bring gifts to children in January. One night, you got up, half-asleep, and stumbled into the kitchen. Thirsty, you opened the refrigerator to look for a glass of milk. And to your astonishment, illuminated by that cold light, there it was—an entire baby pig, with its eyes closed. It seemed to be asleep, like in that children's story, remember? But this one was dead. You were bewildered. What was this poor little animal doing in the refrigerator? Feeling pain and fear, you slammed the door shut. You ran to your sister Adela's room and tried to wake her up. Your temples were pounding, and your heart was beating hard. Adela finally woke up and angrily muttered that she would go to the kitchen with you. When you opened the refrigerator door, she also jumped back, but it was more out of pity than fear. Early the next day, the two of you took the piglet out of the refrigerator and gave it a Christian burial in the garden. You buried it with flowers and prayed for the poor thing. That evening, when your mother asked about the pig that she was going to cook for Christmas dinner, you and Adela—accomplices—barely looked at each other.

The baked skin has that crunchy consistency that is neither hard like pork rinds nor soft like the skin of boiled chicken. The texture is perfect, which is due to that supple fat that adheres to those tiny, soft bones. There is nothing as tasty as sucking, one by one, on those tiny ribs. Fortunately, the waiter left the entire bottle of wine on the table, and whenever he's not looking, you refill your glass to ensure that you be able to take more sips of wine after each bite.

While you chew and sip away during the entire meal, you haven't been able to look away from the mirror. Her open smile has returned a youthful luster to your gray and once again abundant head of hair. You feel your blood flowing freely through your veins, almost with a rush, as if you had violently removed your tie, belt, and socks.

Except for the tiny bones, you clean your plate. But there's still more than a half bottle of wine left. Even though you don't want to drink any more wine, you pour some into your glass and drink it up, because, as your mother used to say, waste not, want not. That's my mom!

Then the waiter brings out a selection of desserts—caramel flan, custards, sweet tarts, baked apples, peaches in syrup. They say that drunks don't eat desserts, but you crave sweets like a child, Juanma. Sporting a dress made by a seamstress, Mommy pulls you along by the hand down the street without letting you stop to look at the marvelous things in the store windows—magic sets, colored pencils, toy soldiers—while right next door at Dulcería Celaya there is a colorful array of candy—multicolored, syrupy, sugary, crystallized, glittering and shiny sweetmeats.

I'll get some candy from Dulcería Celaya, you respond sententiously to the waiter and request a cup of coffee and a snifter of brandy. I'll have Carlos I, please. This is no bar, it's a restaurant. I'm not just drinking, but eating a meal. And if that's what we're doing here, then you must begin with an aperitif and end with a digestif. You decide to leave the wine bottle almost half full. Your Mommy pulls you down the street. You can still feel her energy and strength, which contrast with the leanness of her flesh. Ah, her hands! Nervous, long, excitable, and more appropriate for work than for caressing; tools, yes, but, from time to time, they were also soft and generous.

While you waited for the coffee and brandy, he decided to smoke your cigar. He reached into your tweed jacket and took out the Montecristo that was wrapped with just a cigar band almost the color of the cigar itself. Delicately but decisively, he removed it. Holding the cigar between his index finger and thumb, he rolled it next to your ear, listening to the dryness of the leaves in order to determine how fresh it was. It sounded like the beginning of fall. Good. Unabashedly, he used his tongue to smooth out the nerve endings of the tobacco leaves. Since he didn't have his special cutter with him—otherwise his jacket would have become a Boy Scout backpack—he bit off the end with his teeth and chewed the residue in his mouth before spitting it out. Never lacking any elegance when performing these formalities, he lit the cigar with a wooden match, as one is supposed to do. This time, his spectator in the ritual was the gray-haired woman. It was wonderful that she has left her hair gray. She doesn't tint it, but displays it as her best inheritance. He praised her age with a long drag on the cigar. The smoke circulated magnanimously from inside his mouth toward his nostrils, a trajectory by which one discovers the equivalent of the clitoris of the pleasure of smoking cigars. How marvelous that her eyelids fall like a curtain before the spectacular scene of her eyes, which have yet to lose their brilliance, the way in which her cheeks and the corners of her mouth come together, still displaying a smile, or the way her in which her neck, like the royal leaves of a palm tree crowning its trunk, displays her age without having sacrificed her pride. She's had no plastic surgery to pull her skin tight behind her ears, to freeze her smile, to convert her nose into two cadaverous holes, or to prevent the flutter of her eyelids. You love her age as your own age begins to diminish—the life lines on the palms of your hands disappear, the reddish spots on your face and the black ones on your lungs vanish, the fillings in your teeth dissolve, the hairs in your nose disappear, your breath has no connection to your liver, the wrinkles around your eyes fade away, as does the gray hair on your chest and the fungus around your toenails, and finally, your nasal passages contract, your ears shrink, and your beard disappears. Suddenly, you get an irrepressible, voracious, barbaric, animal-like erection, as if all the semen that you have dispersed in your lifetime has returned to your testicles.

The woman stood up. She was noticeably tall, and despite her years, she still exhibited a magnificent figure. She wasn't too thin, so she must have a solid build, like the Archpriest would have preferred—wide hips, tall (taller than you would have thought when she was sitting down), and excellent carriage. She looks at you. For the first time, she looks right at you without the help of Cupid, the mirror. You desperately want to stand up, say hello, and follow her to the restroom, but as if you were a bashful adolescent, you stop yourself. Well, now you are an adolescent—thin, angular, not athletic, but firm and bony. And timid, like a jerk. The cigar has begun to irritate you, so you put it out. You leave the brandy untouched—it's like fire anyway. Following behind the woman, you stand up and walk toward the restroom. Relaxed, you run your fingers across the mosaic tiles on the walls while you wait for her outside the door. You're wearing boxer shorts, white socks, and patent-leather shoes. Twelve tiles run the length of the wall. As you count them for the fourth time with your fingers, she comes out of the restroom. You look at her with transparent eyes, and she looks at you tenderly, smiles, bends over slightly, and nervously caresses your head with her long, excitable, soft, and generous hands. Then she affectionately pinches you on the cheek. Taking you by the hand, she guides you to Dulcería Celaya, lovingly.

The famous "rompope" punch made with rum, milk, eggs, sugar, and spice was always the best. But, in addition, there was "cajeta de Celaya," made of sweetened condensed milk and traditionally packaged in round, brightly colored thin wooden boxes with gold tags and tiny drums on top. And golden honey, Christmas candies, guava, pitted sugared dates, sugared fig-leaved sweets, oranges, sugared pumpkin, glazed figs, candied biznaga cactus, strawberries, peaches, apricots, pears in syrup, wrapped, candied sweet potato cut into bars and marzipan, nougat, gumdrops, caramel, sugar-glazed nuts, macaroons, pumpkinseed fudge, Mexican wedding cookies, meringue-filled deep-fried scones, aniseed cookies, candy eggs, amaranth candy, chocolate truffles, sweet nuts from Coahuila and Nuevo León, caramelized nuts, sliced candied fruit, candied almonds, pine nut fudge, nut candy kisses, Mommy, please, toasted sweet amaranth seeds in plastic bags, Mommy, please, teardrops, Mommy.

CHAPTER 5

Savoring the drowsiness brought on by the wine and chewing on some pumpkin seed wafers from Dulcería Celaya that reminded him of his First Communion, Juan Manuel retraced his steps back to Cinco de Mayo and the Miguel Ángel stationery store. Amid a thousand fountain pens in the store window—Aurora, Montblanc, Parker, Rialto, Sheaffer, Cross, Sirocco, Pelikan, Dupont, Delta, Omas—he saw it. Resting in its new case, coveted yet out of reach, flamboyant, octagonal, magnificent, was the pen of his dreams. Breathing on the windowpane, he contemplated it with veneration, as if it were a sacred instrument. It must be God's pen.

He had always been enthralled with fountain pens. And with ink, too. It fascinated him—even terrorized him—to think that the pen's ink cartridge could contain the book that the pen would inevitably write. For some time now, he had been using the computer in his office for academic purposes, but at home he would write his notes, letters, and personal items by hand with his stubby, sacred Montblanc Meisterstuck, a true classic that he'd had for years, long before that widespread duty-free promotion had allowed so many pen pushers to acquire them legally. In reality, it was a simple object—a tube filled with a black liquid that came to a point on one end. The fountain pen produced the miracle of writing. In fact, it represented an even greater miracle, that is, language, a system of codes that's ordinary yet complex and mysterious, so comprehensible in everyday practice, yet incomprehensible as a quintessential talent or trait.

Despite a shaky pulse that caused him to waver, his handwriting was not only delicate, but also energetic. And his footsteps, those that he was taking now as he walked around the center of the city, were they not in effect the stuttering—or inebriated—calligraphy that someone was dictating without his having anything to say about it?

Now he was tired and sleepy. And he could still feel that same sensation which felt like his brain was too large for his skull. Nevertheless, he had to stick to his itinerary, which he did, ever so slowly now, heading down Cinco de Mayo toward the Zócalo.

The sun was behind him now, and it was shining on the cathedral's western steeple, making it look like a freestanding tower at the far end of the street. It stood next to the back side of the Monte de Piedad pawnshop, where the reddish color of the porous volcanic rock walls seemed to evoke Aztec sacrifices and the suffering caused by the Inquisition. Where are you headed, Juan Manuel? Why don't you just go home and take a nap in order to reduce that swelling of your eyelids.

But there was no turning back. The calligraphy guiding his path told him to cross the street and make his way toward Café La Blanca, El Fénix Drugstore, Miguel's Luggage Store—he's the best salesman ever—Hotel Washington, and, inevitably, as far as La Puerta del Sol Bar. Then he needed to urinate again.

Suddenly, just as Juan Manuel walked into La Puerta del Sol and as if the open wounds of the volcanic rock had healed over, the already tenuous, smog-ridden afternoon light simply vanished. In essence, La Puerta del Sol was nothing but the scab of an old wound.

Not many people were inside. It was that slack time of day when a few rounds of drinks slowly evolve into a late afternoon lunch—bean soup, pickled fish, pig's feet in vinaigrette sauce. Having already said to hell with the rest of Friday, the only ones who were there were the ones who were always there at that hour, already consumed by drink, dominoes, and inane conversation.

Juan Manuel placed his umbrella on a nearby chair, not simply to claim a place to sit down, which wasn't necessary because there were lots of open tables, but mainly to give the idea that he had gone into the bar for more than taking a pee. I'm leaving my umbrella on consignment, and he headed straight for the restroom. After urinating with a sonorous sigh of relief, he needed another drink.

So, what are you going to order? Whatever you choose now will determine your destiny. Another shot of brandy would complement the digestif that you had after consuming wine at Bar Alfonso. Fermented grapes are generous, but they're not to be mixed with other types of alcohol. If you order another brandy by itself, as it should be, or perhaps along with a bottle of mineral water, you won't satiate your thirst; inevitably, you'll end up ordering two or three more. You could get a scotch and soda, but that's for stimulating conversation, and your students are nowhere to be seen. They let you down, Juan Manuel. You're all alone now. Whom are you going to talk to? Scotch is just going to make you sluggish. Since you're already sleepy and tired, you'll end up falling asleep with your head on the table, and you won't even have talked to yourself. While gin is more stimulating, you don't have a high tolerance for it like scotch. And you wouldn't be able to abide by the calligraphy that's determining your itinerary either. However, after a gin and tonic, that calligraphy would come to an abrupt end, right in the middle of a sentence. Due to the intervention of free will and luck, which are already written somewhere else, it would stop in a splotch of ink on a half-finished page. No, dear Segismundo, it won't be like that. Oh, you poor devil, you're so pitiful. Okay, then, a rum and Coke. It's invigorating, passionate, and tropical. So, why not a mixed drink, a rum and Coke?

However, you end up ordering another shot of brandy. You're trying to convince yourself that it's the natural corollary to your meal and not the beginning of stage two of your tour, which you want to delay as long as possible. Carlos I brandy, your second Carlos I—well, it's your Carlos II. If the first one conferred upon you the emperor's attributes of conqueror, the second one could leave you sickly, weak-willed, insane, and bewitched. You're going to go from displaying the grace of Titian's equestrian portrait to the morbid images in paintings by Carreño de Miranda. There was that look of idiocy; long, mangy hair; slobbering, protruding jaws; puffy eyelids; transparent cheeks daubed with a thin film of false color done by one of the waiters or the painter himself.

From your corner table, you look around: hardly anyone is there. You count them. Seven. Just men. Seven machos. That's the way they smell.

Displaying looks of serious professional concentration at one moment, then open, vulgar exaltation at another, four of them are caught up in a game of dominoes. You can hardly distinguish their heads. Sitting at another table, two stubborn, feisty guys are bantering back and forth—without listening to each other—peppering their words with that eternal drunken stuttering. The last person is a heavyset guy standing at the bar with one foot on the railing above the garbage strewn about from earlier customers. For no reason, he looks at you with some friendliness, ready to crack a smile. But then he peers back into his glass, observing the liquid that gives him comfort and solace while it continues to disappear.

A balding, child-like guy from Asturias, who is the bartender, skims a popular newspaper while he runs his fingers, now practically frozen from continually putting ice in glasses, over the curvy lines of the seminude Nordic models on page three in order to warm them up.

The place is deader than a doornail—four guys are playing dominoes, now unable to talk sensibly, others argue heatedly, another drinks alone, and the bartender is running his fingers over a magazine as if it were Braille. You look at all of them.

You could be somewhere else, but you're here because of that unintelligible calligraphy that forces you to remain at La Puerta del Sol, drinking your second brandy, your Carlos II. Absolutely nothing is going on, and nothing is going to happen either. What the hell are you doing here? What a waste of time! Once and for all, why don't you just go home?

By now, you know who won the domino game. You've already obliquely heard the emphatic repetition of a series of monologues by the two guys who are pretending to talk to each other. You've already imagined the life and trouble of the fat guy drinking alone at the bar, and you've already imagined the bartender's erotic day-dreaming, which doesn't quite make him a pervert. What else is there, Juan Manuel? You could just knock back the rest of your Carlos II, as if it were a shot of tequila, leave the bar, get swept up by the late-afternoon crowds, and go home. However, even though continuing to walk doesn't appeal to you, returning to your domestic disaster appeals even less. You really want to have another drink, but you want to drink it slowly so that you can savor the flavor and take pleasure in the delicate filaments of its composition, swirling it around under your tongue and circulating it on top to bring heat to your palate.

Despite the tequila, beer, and food, you haven't quite cured yourself of that lingering hangover. You could use some help right now. What if you call Antonio? Or Fernando? No. There must be a reason why they didn't come today. Drinking bouts can be friendly, happy, and celebratory, but hangovers are experienced by doing penance in isolation.

Stuck to the wall, a television set drones insipidly. The liquor bottles, like patient prostitutes, await their customers. The cash register, now a relic, guards its treasure in silence. Happiness and satisfaction permeate the image of Johnny Walker.

Next to the bar, behind the fat guy who was drinking alone, there was a small glass case with a collection of old paper money. Brandy in hand, Juan Manuel stood up. Although unnecessary, because theoretically there was enough space between him and the guy standing at the bar, he still signaled an "excuse me" to the solitary man, since in reality he knew instinctively that the guy needed more space than he had calculated. Without saying anything, the man smiled and moved aside.

You are unaware that you look senile as you put on your glasses. You examine the images on the collection of money that pertains to your youth: the Angel of Independence; the provocative gypsy laden with beaded necklaces; the smiling girl from Tehuantepec; Josefa Ortiz de Domínguez, always in profile; Ignacio Allende, sporting long sideburns and a two-cornered hat; Miguel de Hidalgo, looking old, tired, hunchbacked, and sighing more than he was proclaiming independence; Morelos, waiting in anticipation; Cuauhtémoc, the bronze race. You try to remember the other side of those bills: the Aztec calendar on the one-peso note; a view of Guanajuato on the 10-peso note . . . or was it the twenty? The national seal on the 100-peso note. You can't remember the others.

Then you feel the piercing stare of the man who is drinking alone behind you. As you turn around, he raises his smudged, finger-stained glass to you. You do the same with your glass. He mumbles something weakly. You respond in kind.

With that simple, reciprocal gesture, a conversation was struck up. The man who was drinking alone had nothing in common with Dr. Barrientos, unless you consider that both men were drinking alone, which at that moment is what most characterized him, and consequently, what identified him with Juan Manuel. At first, Dr. Barrientos rejected the idea of initiating a conversation with him, so he just mumbled something in response as he began to return to his table, realizing initially that he had just finished his second Carlos I. What the hell are you going to talk about, anyway? You have nothing to say to him. You have nothing in common with him, no ideas, and, clearly, neither the same language nor even the same habits. However, it turned out that Juan Manuel didn't return to his table; instead, trapped by the only topic that could ever surface under those circumstances—that is, the very drink that each man was imbibing in solitude and the same conversation that was always changing their lives—Juan Manuel, between drinking alone and now with him, ordered another Carlos I, now the third one that was supposed to end his hangover and give him a new lease on life, which was like going from the Austrian dynasty to Bourbon rule.

What the hell's wrong with you, Juan Manuel? Always so reserved, selective, and protective of your space and intimacies, here you are talking to this unknown person, who has dirty fingernails and a protruding belly, totally seduced by his friendly smile and his unconditional willingness to have a drink with you in this insipid bar. Patiently, he listens to you. He doesn't butt in or act surprised at your confessions, because you begin at the end of your life, with a confession. In addition, you still feel the humility caused by the hangover, to the point that the first thing you confess is precisely the fact that you have a hangover and that you feel like crap. And from that opening declaration come feelings of resentment that would be hard to reveal even to an old friend, but ones that you can divulge to this fat stranger, who is already putting his hand—with dirty fingernails—on your shoulder. So, you confess: you're on the edge of giving up hope; your students have abandoned you; and you don't want to go home, because this morning as you were getting dressed—blue jeans, tweed jacket, argyle socks, dark red Italian loafers—you discovered, terrified, that there was a dead body in your closet and no one you could call for help.

Once you have managed to articulate your bitterness, you cross the line from feeling hungover to being drunk. Now you feel better. Your Carlos III wakes you up and you feel livelier. You even smile sarcastically like some enlightened despot.

You give a toast to Salvador, that's his name, he says, and you clink your glass with his, as if you were old friends from childhood, but not for things you had in common, but rather for having shared a common territory, like the same block, neighborhood, or school.

Like Uriarte, the rich kid of the class, who was an only child, the heir apparent, the one living in that mansion in San Miguel with the summer home in Cuernavaca. You haven't talked to any of those kids since then. You've never even exchanged a word with them, and none of them has ever been a part of your life. And here you've spent your entire life saying words, writing them, wasting them, and squandering them. Despite the fact that those guys were all so different, once you had prepared for First Communion together, the neighborhood and the school had made them accomplices. You shared the same pew during the moments dedicated to purity, the venial and mortal sins, the last years, death, hell, and eternity. That is to say, beginning with Genesis, you had shared the meanings of blame, fear, the fascination with evil . . . even though you always took things more seriously than Uriarte. Even though your family's economic status was quite distinct from his, you were also neighbors living on the same block. Do you remember the first time you went to his house? You hadn't been invited, but you decided to go anyway. Still not tall enough to reach the doorbell, you touched the buzzer with your baseball bat. While trying to contain a German shepherd that was jumping up and putting his paws on your chest, the girl—a euphemism for aging female servants—let you in. After crossing through a vestibule with a gold-framed mirror and a tall round table with a vase of flowers in the middle, you practically stumbled into that colossal salon. Directly above a Persian rug, a sad-looking chandelier hung from the ceiling, which was twice as high as the room was wide. Until then, the word *salon* was unknown to you except as some French term, as were the words *chandelier* and *Persian*. You were astounded by the luxury and size of the huge room. A short time later, Uriarte appeared below one of the arches of the tall cloister and greeted you with a strange "What's up?" Then he descended what looked like a movie version of a staircase that spiraled upward to the first floor. You spent the entire day with Uriarte. You even had dinner in that oh-so-elegant dining room, where you did battle with all that silverware, crystal water glasses, and large cloth napkins that they kept laying across your lap. At nightfall, you headed home. That was a big day: you played with the dog long enough to lose your fear of him; you spoke your first swear words, which until then embarrassed you when you heard them; you played on the roof terrace; and you got inside the Oldsmobile that was in the garage, sat in the driver's seat, and played with the gearshift and the lights. Uriarte showed you the best hiding places in the entire house, and he let you play with his toys—boxing gloves, toy rifle, sword, pistols, fire truck, skates, electric train. After playing cowboys, pirates, sword fighters, boxers, and cops and robbers, you left the house together and went down the street toward your house. He wanted to be with you right to the end—with an arm over each other's shoulder—like now, in La Puerta del Sol, and without saying much, you became friends for life, acknowledging the implications of loyalty and envy that came with the turf. Just about everything you had done for the first time in your life was with Uriarte. He was your accomplice in your First Communion, first lie, first field trip, first beer, and first all-nighter. With him you went for the first time to a circus, an adult movie, a party, and a bar. With him, you learned how to play pool, to shave, and to drive a car. With him, in Cuernavaca, you got drunk for the first time, while at the same time—unbeknownst to you—your father was dying. Uriarte is your first history and geography course, and he's right here with you now, at your side in this dive, giving you a good-bye hug at the bus stop on your way home, after seeing a movie together. This guy's too fat, and his fingernails are dirty. And you have a dead body in your bedroom closet.

Later on in life, there were the other friends with whom you had things in common, such as similar likings, interests, and values. It had been like a Second Communion.

The day after your father was buried, you went to school as if—for the first time—you were an orphan. You wanted the world to feel sorry for you. Your first hangover still lingered, triggering an unwarranted amount of resentment that had remained a part of you for the rest of your life. You were sad and confused. No matter how many times you repeated that your father was dead, you were unable to accept—without any warning or preparation—the truth of what had so suddenly imposed itself upon you. It had become a nightmare from which you were unable to free yourself and in which you were inextricably trapped. According to your height, you would take your place in line at school. Villegas, who would line up behind you because he was slightly taller, approached you just as the school principal shouted in military fashion to mark distances, meaning that each student had to raise his right arm and put it on the shoulder of the student in front of him. Villegas disobeyed the order and whispered into your ear: I know how you feel. He didn't say it at an arm's distance, or from behind, or with just one arm, but with both arms. Hugging you right in the middle of formation, from that moment he had broken ranks to join you . . . forever.

Villegas had been the new guy in class. If he hadn't had a strong personality, he would have become the brunt of jokes and probably paid dearly for it. However, he had a penetrating look of intimidation that made him seem more like an adult than an adolescent. Several months after your father died, he invited you to his house for dinner. You left school together, and instead of walking to the bus stop, he took you to his car, a Valiant Barracuda that popped your eyes out. Although you climbed into the car as if it were an everyday occurrence, you were also surprised that he had the keys to his parents' apartment, because to get into your house you still had to ring the doorbell. You had learned that his father had died a couple of years earlier—I know how you feel, he had said—and you were expecting to meet a sorrowful and severe widow like your mother at his house. However, aside from a servant in an overly starched dress, there was no one to be seen in that luxurious residence. This library has eleven thousand volumes, said Villegas quantitatively, while you looked on qualitatively. There were only two place settings at the dining room table. As Villegas offered you a sherry, you sank down into a sumptuous black leather chair that in effect initiated you into the world of adults that included olives, dainty napkins, and the music of Chopin coming from the record player. After you were sitting down at the table, the servant served you on the left and picked up on the right. After taking a sip of the wine, Villegas pronounced three or four adjectives that would have been more appropriate for describing people than the wine. During the meal, the two of you discussed literature and talked about books that had been censured by the church, after which you collectively created your own reading list. Nearing the end of the meal, but before dessert was served, you were surprised when a selection of cheeses that you had never eaten before was placed on the table. They had a strong smell, no, they stank. Imagining them walking off by themselves, you deduced that the worse they smelled, the better they tasted. After dessert, Villegas served you almost simultaneously an espresso, a snifter of Cardenal Mendoza brandy, and a Cuban cigar . . . your first espresso, your first brandy, your first Cuban cigar. In order to maximize your enjoyment of them, he suggested that you retire to a smaller sitting room. Then Villegas sat down at the piano and played the same song by Chopin that you had heard on the record player. You had no words to express your amazement at all these things. You had no idea that brandy could have different categories of dryness, that you could put a tiny piece of lemon rind in the coffee, and that you had to remove the paper ring from the cigar before lighting it. And what could be said about Chopin and Villegas's rendition of it?

Although he was your age, Villegas lived alone. After his father died, his mother married again and bought her son an apartment directly below theirs, where a servant took care of his every need and where they had put the thousands of books that had belonged to his deceased father.

Although Villegas didn't enroll in San Ildefonso High School like you did, outside the classroom you still shared that era encompassing everything from Hermann Hesse to the existential philosophers, from the Violines Mágicos to Elvis Presley, from the immaculate virgins to the whores in the Nápoles neighborhood, and from those legendary days then to La Puerta del Sol today, in order to help you remove that cadaver that you had found in your closet this morning. Obese and slovenly, the man accompanies your Carlos III, quietly but letting you know he understands, just an inch or so from your nose, with that foul-smelling breath.

You had enrolled at a university without your friends, because they had decided to pursue professions that guaranteed a future, such as law, medicine, or engineering. You were the only one of the entire group to enroll in liberal arts, which is how you came to meet Federico: so many ideas, so many dreams, head and heart in unison, all of which started to unravel and become intertwined with your own dreams during those innumerable afternoons that evolved into nights and nights that multiplied into early morning hours—the poem committed to memory and reconstructed line-by-line; the record that was replayed twenty times over drinks that proliferated infinitely; the commonplace references from which humor emanates; those simultaneous discoveries that tickle your happiness; and those euphoric affinities that become retroactive. You tell him about the cadaver that you discovered in your bedroom closet—the extended arm, as if he were begging for help, the blood trickling from one corner of his mouth, that blank stare. Federico gives you a hug from the side, because his voluminous belly prevents him from hugging you straight on.

And your students never showed up. Even if they had arrived late, they would have been able to track you down in one of those bars. Antonio had been with you many times, and he would have known any alternate routes that you might have taken. Due to the miracle of a generous calligraphy, your oldest and best friends are those who are with you and the ones who are willing to take care of that dead body.

They step back from the bar where they have been chatting for a good part of the afternoon, and like a uterus enveloping and protecting them, they take a seat on a straight-backed, semicircular bench at a table. They don't know each other, but the three of them—Uriarte, Villegas, Federico—toast each other and do the same to you. You're their common denominator. You come together, meet each other, tell stories, laugh out loud like children, hug each other, and have another round of drinks. According to the topic that repeatedly excludes one of the three, two by two you talk about literature, politics, sickness, travel, alcohol, friends, enemies, and aging. Happy, smiling, you listen to them talk. You're the interlocutor that each one of them prefers, because you settle their disputes and you make the final judgment as to who is right. Despite their right to be there, no women are present, but they end up being the preferred topic of choice anyway.

You don't want to think about Alejandra. Her image, which you try to reject, invades your thoughts and makes your body ache. You drive her from your soul with a gesture that escapes through your hands; in her place, Jimena overtakes your imagination and dominates you, similar to that morning in your office when her smile illuminated the brutal darkness of the irreversible departure of Alejandra. You make a toast to Jimena. You think for the *n*th time how much you would've enjoyed her company on this outing. You envisage how intently she would've followed your umbrella as you pointed at some cornice, pinnacle, or vaulted niche, but more important, how much she would have followed the secret advances of your desire. Invoking her name, you're suddenly overtaken by an ill-founded but firm premonition that Jimena will be waiting for you in the Zócalo at the very moment the flag is taken down. They don't take flags down, you correct yourself, they lower them. What a rich language, especially those verbs symbolizing the concept of nation—to raise a flag, to wave a flag, to lower a flag. And Jimena at the center, the very center of the Zócalo, next to the flagpole, waiting for you, all of which is made real by the powers of your imagination—her coarse voice and catlike gestures—which send shivers down your back. Will she come alone, or with a friend or lover? And what if she comes with Antonio? Given that he looks at her so much in class, can she have become involved with him? Or with Fernando? No, not with Fernando. Although he's charming, he can't hold a candle to her, not even a tiny one. Even though they're probably the same age, next to her he's like a child. Jimena would never fall for him. Enlightened, you swallow your jealousy along with your Carlos III. Like a shot of tequila, you knock it back and begin to wait for Jimena to arrive on that date you've evoked in your imagination. In order to attenuate your desire to have her at your side, you order your Carlos IV, the one that will make you pudgy, ridiculous, cowardly . . . and a cuckold. Without saying anything, you toast Salvador, who takes up half of the bench and orders a glass of multifaceted rum—Bacardi, white, abundant, straight, but with a Coke and mineral water on the side.

Pondering the possibility of Jimena going out with just any son-of-a-bitch, you wanted to take her captive and seduce her. Watching her unfold and ripple, you raise her on the flagpole in the Zócalo and render military homage, whistling the national anthem all the while. She's the flag, you're flagpole. With each drink, you begin to recuperate your dispersed energy, but you still feel like the kid who was lured into Dulcería Celaya—with your wafer stuck between your teeth, with her candy stuck between your teeth, seeking the heart of sex, making it, actually: rising and fluttering—Here's to life!—but it's coming to an end.

There is no Carlos V, because he was the first.

With some difficulty, Juan Manuel said goodbye to Salvador, who wanted to have just one more drink, honest, just one more for the road. He paid the bill for both of them and set out walking toward the main plaza, where he was sure that Jimena was going to be waiting for him.

As Juan Manuel walked out of La Puerta del Sol Bar, he heard Salvador, "Don't worry, I'll take care of that dead body," but Juan Manuel didn't hear the last part:

"In fact, I've already taken care of it."

CHAPTER 6

By then, the day was starting to wane. Leaving La Puerta del Sol, Juan Manuel started walking nostalgically toward the west steeple of the cathedral, the same one that continued to persevere in solitude at the end of the street.

As soon as he arrived at the city's main plaza, the Zócalo, he looked at the flagpole with anxiety. It was bare, nothing seemed to be moving, only a thick, amorphous cloud—like a gigantic miasma—hung over the plaza. Of course, Jimena was not there. The Zócalo seemed larger than ever before, grayer than ever, and like no time ever before, it was completely deserted.

Dr. Barrientos stationed himself near one corner of the atrium of the cathedral, at the base of the steeple, along with dislocated columns of yet older columns that in the distant past had been a part of not only the principal church that Hernán Cortés had ordered built not long after the Conquest, but also the stones of the ancient Aztec temple dedicated to Tláloc and Huitzilopochtli. After the devastation of the Great Tenochtitlan by Cortés' armies, the monoliths of the sacrificial temple were reduced to octagon shapes of Hispanic columns that provided the base of the church that was built by the conqueror on top of the ravaged Temple of the Sun. Constructed with the speed and modesty required by the circumstances at hand, that church was, in turn, destroyed as soon as the ostentatious desires of the religious establishment could manage to replace it. Some of the stones that at one time were a part of pre-Hispanic construction are still conserved there, alongside the steeple on the west side, bearing the markings of the reptilian plumage of Quetzalcóatl. Among those shattered columns that served as a pedestal, King Cuauhtémoc, with a bronze gaze that mirrored the hyperboles of his race, contemplated a plastic wreath recently placed in front of his bust by humble hands.

With affection, you study the young man, now an aging statue . . . yet a heroic inspiration of art. You mimic his look—wrinkled eyebrows, jaws pressed together, gazing into the distance—but no matter how much you gesture, you can't help but exude the same feeling of defeat as the eagle spiraling precipitously into the abyss.

Following the trajectory of King Cuauhtémoc's gaze, you're intimidated by the imposing steeple of the cathedral. You decide to view it like the plucked eagle would've seen it, from the bottom up, meticulously, at your own speed, as if you were undressing Jimena, starting with her shoes and ending with the ribbon in her hair. You want to go over her little by little, without letting even a single detail—an adornment, her outline, a mole, a scar—escape you.

The entire history of the cathedral is contained in that single steeple, that is, the successive stages of its construction, once erected upon the ruins of the Temple of the Sun of the Great Tenochtitlan, then on top of the rubble of the first cathedral. Musingly, you think that this city is like an onion, and so your eyes begin to look upward, peeling away the layers of history starting at ground level, which is slowly sinking. The foundation—enormous, impregnable, and not unlike the severity of El Escorial in Spain—is a virtual fortress. Jimena's legs, long but steadfast:

Oh, pedestals of marble, living edifice
Built with heaven's artistry,
Alabaster columns that on earth
Give us a sign of the Almighty!

Those who began the construction of the cathedral knew full well that it would not be finished during their lifetimes; hence, they challenged future generations to one day finish that steeple. Judging from the dimensions of its base, it seemed to have been meant to reach the sky, not unlike the Tower of Babel. As a result, subsequent generations exhausted their imagination and talents in the continuing construction of the steeple, making each new stage even more graceful and nimble, but without losing its harmony and continuity with respect to its base. In effect, thanks to the architect at the time, who designed five arches on each flank and created those inverted, gyrating, scroll-shaped brackets that unite the bodies of the steeple with feigned spontaneity, the second stage is narrower and less voluminous. Such marvelous hips, Jimena, and a similarly incredible waist. It's impossible that this minuscule space embraces your stomach, liver, pancreas, kidneys, gallbladder, and intestines, that is, the main part of the body, including the ardor of love:

Beautiful spires and artifice
of the arch that makes me jealous!
Altar where the young tyrant god
sacrificed himself!

You wield your umbrella like a sword and with its support you reproduce the uncommon spirals of jutting stone that, instead of providing support, sustain an inversion. This cathedral, you declare out loud, has to be viewed upside down. Pedestrians note sarcastically that you're missing a marble or two, but some gather to watch your ridiculous contortions, because then you do an about-face from the steeple in order to demonstrate your assertion. Without bending your knees and guided by a precarious equilibrium, you bend straight over as far as you can and put your head between your knees. Now converted into a triumphal arch, you can see in topsy-turvy fashion the steeple of the cathedral. You imagine that the sky is the ground, while the foundation stands out from the gargoyle-laden protruding supports. Now somewhat dizzy and about to stumble, you manage to stand up straight. Still lucid enough to continue your explanation of the third and last stage, you explain that it's even more audacious than the second one: the architect, having perforated the steeple with spaces to hold twenty bells, thought that it was important to give an additional feeling of airiness to the weighty structure; thus, he decided to inscribe an octagon within a square, giving the third stage, now ventilated, the illusion of hanging in air. Your supple waist, Jimena, your delicate breath, and your fluffy hair. And to top it off, a stone bell that confuses content with the continent makes the steeple as precarious as the bells themselves:

> Oh, the portal of the glory of Cupid
> Guardian of the most treasured flower
> of all there is and has been in the world!
>
> Let us know how long you will be closed
> and the crystalline sky will be defended
> from whomever tasted that prohibited fruit.

Dr. Barrientos gave a heavy, tired sigh. Seconds later, once again he scrutinized the entirety of that steeple, from the foundation to the cross at the top. During this momentary visual appraisal, three centuries of history had elapsed.

Even though the sun was starting to go down, the temperature remained the same. Wanting to rain, it was hot and sticky outside.

Not having the strength to sustain a face-to-face confrontation, Juan Manuel refused to walk in front of the cathedral. One steeple had been enough, so he walked along the western side of this imposing structure and through the rectory amid the garbage dumped into a flower bed, along the sides of which couples trying to make out had discovered a secret refuge. From there he went to Guatemala Street, which during pre-Hispanic times had led to the main temple of the Aztecs and during the colonial period was called Las Escalerillas. Walking in the shadows on the north side of the cathedral, he headed in the direction of the great sacrificial temple.

Among the religious artifacts in the storefronts up ahead, the saints—before turning in—gave him their blessings: Saint Martin of Porres, whose stark white eyes contrasted with the shiny blackness of his face; Saint Philip of Jesus, with two lances piercing his body while maintaining a smile; Saint Anthony, a monk ready to stand on his head amid the clamor of unmarried women; Saint Joseph, so very chaste—poor guy!—holding a bouquet of white lilies; and even the Virgin of Guadalupe, ready to shed the splendor she has worn like a cape forever and ever. Up and down the street, the metallic storefront shutters began their noisy and relentless descent, decapitating those saintly gazes . . . Good-bye, Juanma, sweet dreams, see you tomorrow. How could you dream of little angels? You were just buried in the darkest darkness of your bed, and feeling the threat of kneeling in a confessional at church, your mother, having blessed you with hurried fingers, turned away and closes the door. Darkness wasn't a co-conspirator of little angels, but rather of the devil. As soon as you fell asleep, he tugged at your feet to take you to hell, or worse, purgatory, where your soul isn't necessarily resigned to eternal suffering, as in hell, but to an indefinite prolongation of a pain that you know is permanent. Although your mother told you to dream about little angels, you couldn't imagine a heaven of angels to be the same luminous blue sky that you saw from down here when you were a young child; instead, it was a dark, cavernous space barely illuminated by a tiny candle that only functioned to confirm the immense darkness of the space.

Before reaching the courtyard at the seminary, Juan Manuel bumped into a folding table with a red-checkered tablecloth on the sidewalk, which greeted and invited him for a drink. Sparklingly fake cocktails with plastic olives and cherries had been poured into glasses on the table of La Casa de las Sirenas Bar. He decided to listen to the sirens' song, and to defy any potential danger lurking outside. In case his ears harbored any waxy buildup, he scraped at his eardrums with his little finger and, feeling excited, walked through the door. He walked down a long, narrow corridor that led to some stairs. He stopped midway to view an encased nineteenth-century German representation of a woman with appetizing breasts. He made it to the top of the stairs. From there, he saw only some tables with the same checkered tablecloths that were awaiting local customers. Not a single other soul was there. Nervously, he looked down the hallways. The fake cocktails on the street had awakened your thirst, Juan Manuel, which is another way of saying that your thirst had never really dissipated. Turning around, he spied in the dark another set of stairs, which were much narrower and made of wood. After climbing the creaky steps, he came upon a much more inviting room that was equally devoid of customers. A long, ample bar protruded from a sidewall. Despite the absence of customers, a drowsy cashier and a thin, woeful-looking, seemingly teetotaling bartender, who could make the perfect martini, were quietly waiting for business. To the back was the bar's terrace, a space that had been sacrificed by the presence of the cathedral and the sanctuary.

You want a martini, Juan Manuel. What do you mean, a martini? Don't you realize that you're alone? Like champagne, martinis are not to be consumed alone; they were invented precisely for toasting, inspiring love, and seducing. What the hell, you're alone but you want a martini, end of discussion. Feeling duped, you nonchalantly ask the bartender if he has Bombay gin and, just in case, Sapphire, as if you were in the Oak Bar of the Plaza Hotel in New York City. Of course, he responds in English, surprisingly. Behind the bar, the bartender inserts a tiny silver key into the lock of a small door and removes that blue bottle with a square base displaying the image of Queen Victoria. Bombay gin is the preeminent symbol of the British Empire because, in addition to the berries of the juniper tree, its perfume comes from exotic fruit, seeds, and bark from distant lands, such as China, Morocco, Java, Africa, and Indochina, that stimulated, among other things, an interest in botany among British subjects. When you ask the bartender if he knows how to prepare martinis the way they're supposed to be prepared, he doesn't respond with words . . . he quickly sets two exemplary cocktail glasses on top of the bar. Why two glasses, you wonder, but you don't even bother to ask. He drops two particularly hard pieces of ice into each glass. Taking each one by the base, he swirls the ice around inside until a frozen vapor clouds the natural transparency of the glasses. Next, he takes out a small, worn bottle that still bears its original brand name and dispenses one single, categorical drop of angostura bitters on top of the ice. Once the ice cubes have been impregnated with the color of iodine and the deep-rooted aroma of the bitters that are subtly transferred to the glass, the magician hurls them into the garbage. Steadying his hand to pour barely a whiff, he takes a bottle of Noilly Prat vermouth, extra dry, of course, which is the same brand that New York gentlemen receive when they are born and carry with them, half-full, to their graves decades later. At that point, you want to explain to the bartender Luis Buñuel's recommendations for making a truly dry martini, that is, the bottle of Noilly Prat should be placed on a windowsill in such a way that a ray of sunlight passes through its contents and miraculously transports its essence to the glass of gin that, off to one side, awaits its impregnation, exactly in the same way the Holy Spirit pierced the hymen of the Virgin Mary; but you fear that the bartender wouldn't make such theological attempts, you find it odd—if not irreverent—that a cocktail would be prepared in its own glass instead of a cocktail shaker. Nevertheless, you don't complain to him, but simply watch how milord, with the steady hand of a miniaturist painter, allows barely a drop or two of Noilly Prat to trickle into the cold, aromatic cocktail glasses. As soon as the golden liquid permeates their surfaces, again he casts the remnants into the garbage can with the same aloofness with which he tossed out the ice cubes laden with angostura bitters. No sooner has he finished this operation than you hear the martial sound of the silver cocktail shaker inside of which every drop of the 47-proof Bombay Sapphire starts to freeze around the extra-hard ice cubes. In a matter of seconds, the clear liquid—thick, consistent, oily—pours elegantly in temperate fashion, not easy to imagine, into the freezing, aromatic cocktail glasses. In other words, the cocktail shaker wasn't used to mix the gin and the vermouth, but only to chill the former. As a result, the cocktail that initiates or culminates the doubtful tradition of mixing drinks all together is the very negation of itself, because the discriminatory mixture strives to eliminate any presence of the weakest part of the mix. It's the mixture that disguises the euphemism pretending to diminish the predisposition to drink only pure gin, which drives mothers to abandon their children and others to execute suicidal pretensions, as well as sending entire populations of cities headlong into catastrophe. Beyond the annoying dispute between those who say a martini should be shaken and those who prefer them stirred, milord doesn't do either—he simply allows the gin to flow in and around the ice cubes, not mixing them but only chilling the gin. He concludes the performance by placing a large lanced olive into the glasses.

Two. There are two cocktails, Juan Manuel.

One. You're just one person, Juan Manuel. You're alone.

Happy hour. It's that hour of the day when they serve two drinks for the price of one. Happy hour. Wouldn't it be nice if you were charged half price for only one drink. No, they serve you two instead. Two cocktails, served simultaneously, one of which, while waiting to be consumed, begins to spoil. It's unfashionable to drink two of them one after another, but it's a custom that the bartender accepts as normal. Nevertheless, you drink only one of them . . . yours. You delicately caress the stem of the glass, as if it were a dancing partner, so that its contents don't lose their icy-cold temperature.

Let's do a tally. So far today, you've had four beers, three tequilas, half a bottle of wine, and four brandies. But you drank only half of the first brandy. Ah, yes, there was the sherry earlier that morning, not counting, of course, what you consumed last night, which continued into the wee hours of today. Amazingly, you still have a steady hand. Studying the silvery color of the martini, you observe the almost invisible golden thread, a vague reminiscence of the bitters, which, like lightning, crosses diagonally through the cocktail glass. Before taking a sip, you sniff the edge of the glass, and its aroma transports you immediately, nonstop, to New York . . . and to Alejandra.

• • • • •

She had been waiting for you in that marvelous suite in the Regency Hotel on Park Avenue. On the one hand, you were a little self-conscious about being there, in the capital of the world, all expenses paid by her, but how else should it have been, Juan Manuel? On the other hand, you were ready to absorb with every pore of your skin the excitement of being in New York City for the first time, not to mention wanting to give Alejandra the utmost of your passion— you were quite restless back then—and to show her your sensitivity, which was completely epidermal. And you were concerned about your reputation, as if it weren't your reputation, but precisely the reputation you had during your youth, the same reputation that could have moved her to choose you, Juan Manuel, the honest person sine qua non, or at least in comparison to others around you who were so irreproachable, choosing you for no other reason than to invite you to New York to make love to you, as if she had always loved you, all of her life. That particular moment now seemed like a dream . . . to be there, in that suite, in New York City, embracing her and telling her, right from the beginning, that it seemed like a dream to be there, in that suite, in New York City, embracing her. And you wanted to be mature, and you told her that you wanted to be mature and accept her generosity without remorse. You weren't being cynical, I'm not cynical, you told her, but you wanted to take up her way of life, respect her independence, I want to be with you whenever you want to be with me, and I'll go away when you want to be alone, you told her. I'm really excited to be here, you said, I'm scared, too, it's confusing, I love you, Alejandra, and you didn't know how to play down the solemnity of your declaration of love that she didn't need to hear but greatly appreciated. She was not accustomed to experiencing such delicate feelings. Kissing her eyes, then her eyelashes, you began to smile, so did she, and then both of you broke out laughing. Your kisses proliferated, down to her neck and then to her shoulders. You both undressed in broad daylight, making love and inaugurating that carpeted, perfumed suite—that safe harbor, so elegant, ah, yes, Juan Manuel, so different from your faculty professor's house, which, despite the next morning's efforts, which were always subverted by your nocturnal excesses from the night before, was always in a state of disarray, Juan Manuel. Nevertheless, at least on that day, they used as their departure point what should have been their destination. They were unprepared to make love—they hadn't consumed any martinis or champagne, there was no alluring conversation, no theater or concert beforehand, no dinner and dancing, not even a gaze at the spectacular skyline of the city; instead, there was only an excess of haste and desire, after which came the climax and a resulting synchronized, jubilant shout to begin all over again, which they proceeded to do. They could have continued without cessation and stayed there all day long in that hotel room—navigating each other's bodies, traversing far and wide on erotic terrain. However, she also wanted to show you New York, something she had been planning for months, perhaps years, even before meeting or getting to know you. Consequently, you curbed your desire, held back discreetly, and managed to contain yourself throughout the rest of the afternoon and a good part of that night. You had held each other in the shower amid almost unconceivable emanations, after which you put on your only tie and sport coat in order to wait on the balcony for Alejandra, where you exhibited an incredibly pleasant smile. Down below, rows of trees and a river of yellow taxis. Across the street, the darkening shadows of Central Park. Behind and above you, the imposing backdrop of enormous buildings that reflected the intense rays of the sun, which still lingered to the west. Forty-five minutes later, Alejandra made her appearance on the balcony. She was wearing an incandescent, airy dress that was as light as her suspended scent, ever so lightly perfumed, all of which to this day continues to awaken pain and bring you to tears. You grasped her two hands, took a step back, and looked at her from head to toe with the enthusiasm of an adolescent who sighs after a passionate kiss of love. So as to avert suspicion, you stood apart, because even in New York City clandestine operations are everywhere. You met a block away from the hotel and began your first walk together in the July heat of New York City. She was forty years old and you were thirty-seven, Juan Manuel. And to think you had felt too old to be in New York for the first time in your life. Now, you remember that you must have been but a kid, and your ideas about relativity make you think, for a moment, that twenty years from now you'll probably think that this moment when you're drinking a martini in La Casa de las Sirenas will also be a part of your youth. But you reject fantasy over the desperation of a person condemned to death. They walked along those civilized streets that imposed their blinking rhythm of "Walk" and "Don't Walk." And, as much as you tried to mask your awe of the skyline, you couldn't help but look up—now totally astonished—toward that amazing number of floors of one building, reaching a point at which your childish imagination failed you. Alejandra led you through Central Park to the Plaza Hotel. Inside, she walked with an air of self-confidence, while you were feeling somewhat perplexed. Passing through the stately vestibule, the luxury and brilliance of which left you once again speechless, you entered the elegant staidness of the Oak Bar, where you ordered your first martini of the trip. At that moment, precisely, you knew that it was true love, the love you had been imagining all those years, those times when it had been shunned from your life, including those terrible times when you were confined to the four walls of a house belonging to a divorced professor and surrounded by excruciatingly long absences and isolated remoteness, despite the occasional fortuitous tryst. You never had expectations. You would never have a future together. Without ever realizing it, throughout all those years there never had been a future. You had only relied on certain expectations and the accompanying passion that the present moment offered you. That afternoon—in the Oak Bar of the Plaza Hotel in New York City—you finally understood. And now, you're almost back there once again with Alejandra. You can hear that familiar, crystalline sharp clink of two cocktail glasses, silver like the gin, blue like the bottle of Bombay Sapphire.

Cocktail glass in hand, you make your way affectedly like some movie star toward the terrace of La Casa de las Sirenas.

As you stand there, the cathedral overwhelms your view. You look up and the amber lights in the steeples blink and light up for you. Frightened, a cloud of bats takes flight from their domed refuge. From that vantage point, the cathedral seems like the stern of a gigantic seagoing vessel. You can't believe your eyes! Between the steeple of the cathedral to the east and the elevated dome of the chapel, the enormous green splotch of hope of the Mexican flag flaps in the breeze, now flying from the flagpole in the Zócalo. It's but an illusion, because you resist believing that her absence was illusory upon your arrival. Absences are never illusory, Alejandra. After the glimpse of green, the breeze blows the white part of the flag into view, followed by a piece of the eagle, winged but lifeless like the young Moctezuma. When the red parts—so patriotically red—come into view, blazing away between the steeple and the dome, with the bats now having taken flight due to the lights in the steeple, an intimate perfume and a woman's hand like the moisture in the air touch your right shoulder.

Being left-handed, Alejandra naturally holds her martini in that hand. It's the same martini that the bartender poured along with yours. It's happy hour. She remains quiet. You feel a fleeting kiss on your cheek. As she smiles to herself from deep down inside, she drops her eyelids as a way to beseech you not to ask her anything. Then she smiles again, this time not from inside but toward herself, not from deep down inside, but only superficially. Stemming from love and knowing it, she clinks her glass with yours, as if you had arrived together, or as if, here, the two of you had a date to meet each other, and you, with anticipation, had ordered not just one but two martinis. You sit at a tall bar table, next to the railing of the terrace, from which the two stone mermaids giving the bar its name stare at the cathedral. You're unable to speak, you don't even have a right to speak. And as her eyes demanded and begged, she asked you not to. And, of course, you look at each other. You're astonished because she's smiling, meekly. Even though you don't speak, you laugh and sing. Well, she sings, or at least you hear her singing, even though she doesn't move her lips; it was as if she were humming a Bach tune through her nose. It's an unarticulated voice—as you sip your martinis—that perhaps doesn't deserve the designation of *voice* per se. She nibbles on her olive with mundane sensuality. Where does that song come from? Is it Alejandra or the mermaids just beyond the railing on the terrace who sing to you, Juan Manuel, a man with a clear mind who is ready to go down with every sinking ship? While you don't ask her anything, you know for sure that she's with you, here, so tangibly present. After you take her left hand with your right, the two of you use your free hands to raise the cocktail glasses and toast each other. "Martinis are like women's breasts, or those of mermaids," declared Dr. Barrientos. "Never more than two; never fewer than two."

You asked for two more martinis, but he brought you four. It's still happy hour. They're perfect, just like the first ones, or like the second ones that, after the Oak Bar, the two of you drank at the St. Regis Hotel, with its elegant mahogany bar and that large painting of that fictitious King Cole sitting on a toilet in front of his accommodating attendants and in front of you and Alejandra, who look at you, with a smile, festive, scatological, and ready— after this martini—to do all the dirty things you can imagine.

You make another toast, repeating the clink of the crystal glasses. She doesn't stop singing, but it's been reduced to humming that is transported to her not-so-maternal breasts on which you'd like to rest your head. You close your eyes. Your head is heavy. You have nowhere to rest it, especially sitting on that barstool. Now your head has become even heavier, but you have nowhere to go. As you turn to either side, you feel like your head is twisting off. If you drop it forward, you'll cut off your breathing; if you drop it backward, you'll block off your trachea.

Why did you die, Alejandra, just like that? Why do I continue talking to you when you're already long dead? Should I talk only about you, about the pain that the scent of your perfume causes me, your friendly smile, your obscenities, and your illegible handwriting? But I can't talk about you. To whom, then, can I talk about you? Whom can I tell about our love affair? No one would understand my being a secret widower. No one would understand this anger that I feel in my heart ever since you died. That's why I talk to you, Alejandra, because you're the only person in the world who is capable of understanding the pain I feel over your death. And when I talk to you about yourself, and you don't hear me or respond, your absence only multiplies, envelops me, suffocatingly, everywhere I go.

It's as if the night itself, or the singing that never ceases, had sucked the vitality of life right out of you, leaving that pain in the chest to travel up to the throat, the nose, into the eyes, now converted into wet humor. You cry—silently, no fuss, no hiccups, no heaving—you simply cry.

Resting your chin on your chest and lacking air, you straighten up momentarily, and before tilting backward, Alejandra's smooth but energetic right hand holds you up while her left hand—even smoother but less energetic—dries your tears with a fine handkerchief, Juan Manuel. It feels clean and smells like starch, like lace with that well-known perfume, now helping you not only to contain your tears but also to renew you. Inhaling the delicacy of its weaving, when it reaches your lips, you kiss her.

In that handkerchief that Alejandra will retain in her loving hands for an eternity are deposited your kisses, your tears, your respiration, your headaches, your face, and your misery.

· · · · ·

You're awakened by the beat of war drums that begins to resonate everywhere, from the Templo Mayor to Seminario Plaza, located between the Metropolitan Cathedral and the National Palace.

On the table, two empty cocktail glasses and four full ones, now watery and warm.

The drums announce the advent of sacrifice.

CHAPTER 7

THE MAIN Temple of Tenochtitlan represents a wound that will never heal. It's a fissure that swallows up the world, a black opening at the center of the Zócalo. At this particular center of the universe, its consubstantial presence is exposed. And behind that devastated pyramid stands the dome of Santa Teresa la Antigua, now tilting to the point of almost falling over. It is as if the venerated saint herself were suspended in the air, miraculously holding it up.

Attracted by the monotonous beating of the drums, Juan Manuel headed toward Plaza del Seminario, where a group of spectators was watching a group of dancers, all of whom were devotees of the Virgin of Guadalupe. Dressed in seashells and wearing feathers in their hair, they carried banners with the image of Our Lady of Guadalupe. Snail shells rattled around their ankles, and women in obscene poses were tattooed on their arms. Their hair was long and sweaty, and they sported T-shirts with transnational logos, blue jeans, and running shoes. They were performing next to a mirror of water between the cathedral and the Templo Mayor that reflected a sad image of an earlier, marshy city. With bloodthirsty eyes, they danced unendingly. War is an everyday affair.

Standing next to the insatiable entry to the old San Ildefonso College, Juan Manuel leaned against a wall of the preparatory school where he had once studied without his friends, paradoxically, at a time in his life when he could have had the greatest number of friends.

This is the Zócalo, your mother had told you. That's the cathedral, she pointed out. And those streets are Seminario, Argentina, Justo Sierra, and San Ildefonso. There, those massive wooden doors, the somber entrance, the monumental interior patio, the three-story arches, and a beehive of students. Previously, you had attended a private, male, religious school. Here, everyone was older, dissimilar, and wore no school uniforms. They were a mix of young men and women, white and brown, adults and—like you—seeming adolescents, rich and poor, extremely poor, where it was possible for the son of a servant to rub shoulders with the son of the president of the republic. Leaning against the walls upstairs, they were all there—talking, laughing, and smoking. As a newcomer, you would take refuge in the oak library that had been put in the old chapel of the school. There, you discovered texts as diverse as the anonymous thirteenth-century *Poem of the Cid* and Pablo Neruda's *Twenty Poems of Love and a Desperate Song*. While that literature might have mitigated your loneliness at the time, it also became your life's destiny.

Even though Juan Manuel had spent several years at that university, even by that time it really wasn't much of a university anymore. The National Preparatory School had become the last redoubt of students who studied in the center of the city. The lawyers had vacated the old, dismal law school. The doctors had abandoned the Court of the Inquisition, which included the gloomy jails of the Perpetua in Santo Domingo Plaza. The engineers had deserted Natural Resources on Tacuba Street. The architects had already left the old San Carlos Academy. The economists had abandoned the romantic mansion on Cuba Street. Upon leaving the area and moving south together to Ciudad Universitaria—the new university that had been built on top of volcanic rock in Pedregal de San Ángel—these disciplines had taken with them the students' boisterousness, laughter, lust, goings-on, and transgressions. With their departure, other entities—eateries, bookstores, boardinghouses, billiard halls, bars, and the odd whorehouse—closed their doors and became submerged in deadly silence. Now, in the hands of bureaucrats wearing shiny suits and Vaseline-laden hair, struggling businessmen, underpaid employees, but without any students other than the handful who remained at San Ildefonso Preparatory School for a few years, the center of the city was sinking into decrepitude. Young Juan Manuel had walked those old streets tirelessly, always looking up at the balconies that at one time possessed an air of majesty about them. Now, all they displayed were barren flowerpots, drooping clotheslines, and rusting propane tanks. Ever since then, the center of Mexico City had provoked in Juan Manuel feelings not only of admiration, but also of anguish. He had been astounded by the opulence of those colonial-era buildings, their highly elaborate stone façades, and their secular history. Nevertheless, he regretted the distortion of their original purpose, the modifications made to their architecture, and the overall degradation. However, thanks to the decadence, he learned to discover the marvels that resulted from the exorbitant mumble jumble of architectural senselessness.

Since there's nowhere to go, you wind your way aimlessly through the sweaty crowd that, not unlike the shell dancers themselves, is not only Aztec in origin, but also made of followers of the Virgin of Guadalupe. Ending up smack in the middle of a crowd of people, each time you stumble you say you're sorry, but also for each word that your memory imposes upon your solitary language.

Beyond the ruins of the Templo Mayor, you could make out the building that later became the Dental School, which was built during the Porfirio Díaz era. However, during convulsive times in 1929, the building was the place where the decree creating university autonomy was signed. Then he chuckled at his bad joke: his "alma mater" had been such a powerful influence on his life that in order to attenuate its importance, he had hoped to change the phrase slightly to "calma, mater," that is, "be calm, Mother," but the university wouldn't buy into that one. Sometime before that yellowish mansion housed the Dental School, the building had been the site of the Royal and Pontifical University of Mexico. It was located at the corner of Moneda and Seminario, and because of some peculiar privilege at the same time, the first bar ever in Mexico City was established there with the name of El Nivel, which, given his preference for being "level," as the name of the bar implies, is exactly what Juan Manuel needed at that point.

Managing to dislodge himself from the growing crowd that the dancers had attracted, he marched off in military step to the beat of the drums toward the bar, which was emitting a barren, dim light under the doorsill of the entrance.

The place is full of people. There's no place to amass, embrace, or give space to your dreams, so you position yourself at the bar in a spot directly in front of the bartender, who is sporting one of those moustaches that looks like nothing more than a thin, black line drawn with an eye pencil above his lip. Hoping to moderate your consumption, you order a scotch on the rocks and a bottle of mineral water. After he sets them in front of you, you mix them together. Even though you're anchored to the bar, you're standing, staring at the bartender's scanty moustache, innumerable bottles, and, through a mirror on the wall, a clock that's going backwards. Well, that's not quite right. It's not that the hours transpire in reverse fashion and each minute is earlier than the previous one, for surely the hands don't go in the same direction as the hands of a watch, but rather in the opposite direction, in the same way the numbers are reversed, so that the eleven is to the right of the twelve and not to the left, and the one is to the left of the two, and so on. Nevertheless, it's a matter of convention that calls into question the certainty of the passing of time, which seems to go backwards, which is to say, one more drink becomes one drink less.

A table became available right next to an improvised cubbyhole under the stairs and a door over which hung a sign—*Ladies*—but the waiters and male clientele were going in and out anyway. With no specific purpose in mind except to daydream a bit, or to remember something from the past—a grudge perhaps—and now that the hands of the clock were really going backwards, Juan Manuel picked up his glass, went to the table, sat down, and took a swig of his drink . . . alone.

There are so many little children in the world who are starving to death, and you won't eat your green beans, your mommy used to say. You can't get up from the table until you've cleaned your plate, she ordered. Determined not to eat those green beans that your young palate detested, somehow you managed to spend the entire afternoon sitting at the table without eating a bite. Similarly, when it came to writing and you were unable to extract anything from your heart to write down, you would apply the same discipline to yourself and repeat with your mother's military voice: Don't write anything if you don't want to, but don't get up from your desk for the rest of the day either. And you complied with your command. You didn't write anything, and you didn't get up from your desk either. You'd just sit there, daydreaming, thinking about other things, like now, sitting at this table in El Nivel, in the company of your scotch, because one fine day you got the terrible idea of writing with a glass of scotch next to you. Soon, those moments of silence would go by more serenely, and at times, when your handwriting became strained and coarse, almost childlike, it was true that the alcohol left you less inhibited and the words would then flow with ease. By the next day, however, the notations in your blue notebook that capriciously registered your hazy comings and goings and were written with an overabundant use of adjectives, were now meaningless. In fact, what at first seemed like audacious twists and turns of the language, exciting phrases, and penetrating imagery, with the humility brought on by convalescence, had turned grotesque and embarrassing, after which you would end up violently ripping out the pages. Later on, there were those days, the afternoons, better yet, the nights when you would sit down at your desk with a drink, but now without your lined notebook, and you would simply drink

. . . and, well, ponder things. That's what you did back then. You're one of those types who can just sit down and ruminate, as if your thoughts don't exist outside of the moment when you conjure them up. In truth, with the justification of first sitting down to write, and, second, collecting your thoughts, you would just sit down to drink instead, of course, in order to let the alcohol open the doors to your daydreams. It was as if the alcohol assisted your writing in speaking about itself while you purposely wrote about writing. A short while later, you would drink to think about drinking while anxiously awaiting the moment to finish your drink and then serve yourself another one, and another one, yet without letting your thoughts pursue any path that didn't involve drinking itself.

Damn! My umbrella.

All of a sudden, Juan Manuel felt naked, exposed to the elements. He couldn't remember where he had left it. At Las Sirenas? At La Puerta del Sol? He couldn't lose it. Alejandra had given it to him in New York. She had bought it at the Met and thought it was cute because the dome of the Sistine Chapel was painted on the inside, including the moment when the omnipotent Father gave life to Adam, the first man, who was given the privilege of never having been a child.

He knocked back his scotch, paid the bill, left a tip larger than the bill itself, and stumbled hastily out of El Nivel.

Outside, the shell dancers continued their routine with apocalyptic fervor, as if it were the last performance of their lives and would lead to annihilation.

In order to find his umbrella, Juan Manuel would have to retrace his steps, climb the stairs of Las Sirenas, and, if it wasn't there, pass through the cathedral and take Cinco de Mayo to La Puerta del Sol. However, instead of going down Guatemala, he decided to go in the opposite direction, on Moneda. Suddenly, due to an urgent necessity, the New York Renaissance umbrella became less important than explaining to Jimena and Fernando that on that street was a succession of the earliest American relics, namely, the first printing press, the first mint, and the first art school.

Not so, Juan Manuel. It's not your desire to teach them about the first artifacts of New Spain that lures you to Moneda. Your students told you to go to hell. Don't you get it? Who in hell are you going to explain the buildings, their history, their architecture to? Yourself? If you go there, Juan Manuel, you'll never come back. Why don't you just go home? At least you've been able to cure your hangover with more alcohol; that is, you've fought fire with fire. Well, eating something helped, too. And the tears, they're better than beads of sweat, because tears clean, purify, and detoxify. You can still go back home right now. Afterward, who knows? If Baldomera didn't clean your place, who cares? You'll just go to sleep, end of story. But there's some superior force, you believe, that's controlling you. It's sending you down Moneda, right? It's as if everything depended on some flip of a coin that you lost forever, long before you were ever born. You like that idea, and here you are on Moneda anyway. But don't be a jerk—that force, if it does exist, is simply an accomplice, an enthusiastic accomplice. Don't laugh, Juan Manuel. You know very well that the gig is up. Now, for sure, the center of the earth is going to tremble. Go home, you jerk. Tomorrow's another day.

"But tomorrow isn't going to be another day," mumbled Juan Manuel, "it will be the same day," and he stiffened his fearful pace along Moneda, as he headed toward La Merced.

Without his umbrella—that pointer, baton, yardstick, chalk, cane—he had suddenly lost some of that professorial look, but he still had his arms and voice. Due to the sinking earth in front of the Archbishop's Palace, he walked down a roller-coaster sidewalk. As he hastily pointed out friezes, spires, and archivolts, the sidewalk was like one big wave, down which nocturnal drunks would stagger. Finally, he came to the end of Primo Verdad, the site of the Great Temple, but then he spotted the small edifice that housed the first printing press in the New World. The building is now lopsided, disproportionate and uneven, with drooping doorways behind which was located the Santa Teresa la Antigua Convent. I'm not inebriated, he mused, the buildings are. They're barely standing up. They were about to sink into the streets that undulated chaotically, as if dark subterranean gods moved them at their leisure. Santa Teresa is drunk, he pronounced happily. The archdiocese is drunk out of its gourd. The cathedral is high as a kite. The Metropolitan Chapel is inebriated. The churches are looped, and the civil buildings and convents are wasted. The city is drunk—the entire city, the bells, the clocks, the staircases, the domes, the belfries, the streetlights, the crosses, absolutely everything—he said euphorically. The only one who is sober is me.

By then, Moneda was dark and mainly deserted, except for some vendors, blind guys, and rats scavenging through garbage left behind by the daily street vendors. He came upon a portable grill on top of which a single corncob was roasting and emitting prehistoric aromas. Three blind men had lined up to buy the remaining cups of Jell-O of their permanently flavorless evening. Poor guys! They don't even realize that Jell-O only tastes like its color. With that, Juan Manuel just kept walking toward La Santísima Church. From the opposite side of the street and standing on the north corner of the National Palace, he could see the ancient Casa de Moneda, the old mint that gave the street its name. Later, it became the Museum of Anthropology, where as a child—and seized with amazement—he saw for the first time the Aztec calendar and the monumental sacrificial stone. He went by the twin palaces named Mayorazgo de Guerrero and observed the sun and moon carved into their fortresslike towers. Upon reaching the metallic shutters of a corner lunch cart, he pointed out to his disciples—with a note of solemnity accompanied by a hiccup—the workshop of the famous folk illustrator and political cartoonist José Guadalupe Posada.

He crossed the street and headed toward the old San Carlos Academy. He informed his students that the Amor de Dios Hospital and been built directly on top of the foundations of that building. The hospital treated people with venereal diseases during colonial times, and its chaplain was none other than Carlos de Sigüenza y Góngora.

Doctor Barrientos would have preferred to talk to Jimena about this intellectual rogue of New Spain, whom he admired so much.

After his expulsion from the Company of Jesus, he held many different positions—some substantial, some wretched, as in the case of Lazarillo de Tormes—in order to support his unswerving curiosity. He was the official cosmographer of New Spain, inspector general of cannons, agent of the Inquisition, chronicler of the archbishop, professor of mathematics at the Royal Pontifical University, principal almoner of Archbishop Aguiar y Seijas. One day, in a state of fury, he destroyed the archbishop's glasses with one fell swoop of his cane. And he just happened to be Sor Juana's confidant. Juan Manuel would have preferred to talk about the man's exploits, for instance, his joy upon contemplating an eclipse with a primitive lens while, at the same time, the inhabitants of the Viceroyalty huddled in churches, believing that this celestial phenomenon was an omen of coming calamitous events and a manifestation of God's ire at everyone's sins; his skill in calming the nerves of the population and alleviating the worries of the viceroy's wife when a comet appeared on the horizon; his rivalry with Father Kino, who, having returned from the Austrian Tyrol, denounced his astrological knowledge as if Creoles walked on two feet out of divine dispensation; his audacity at putting twelve Aztec deities on top of the triumphal arch that was placed in Santo Domingo Plaza for greeting the new viceroy; his gallantry and love of literature and history demonstrated by his throwing himself upon a bonfire in order to save some valuable documents stored in the archives of the town council that were set afire during an uprising; and his sense of modernity when he included in his will that his body, plagued by gastric problems, be donated to science after his death. However, Juan Manuel explained none of this to Jimena, because not only his ideas had become entangled somewhere between his mind and his tongue, but also, out of nowhere, he had stumbled upon La Potosina, a deplorable dive that even at that late hour harbored a couple of clients—more asleep than awake—sitting at the bar. Among the water pipes lining the wall, he spotted a Johnnie Walker advertisement, so he ordered another drink. As it was being poured, he walked back to a minuscule restroom that lacked a urinal. After emptying his bladder in a pestilent hole in the ground, he went back and sat down at a table with a Formica top sporting a beer advertisement—Cervecería Modelo—after which he initiated a one-on-one conversation with the darkly golden glass that had been put in front of him.

You're at it again, seated once again at a small table, having a drink, and forgetting the moment at hand, just like your father, who was always seated at his desk reading the newspapers, only to forget what he'd just read. You also feel like a text that's already been read by someone who can't remember what he's read: not even your students, who didn't join you on the tour today; not your friends, who have been evaporating in your binges, just like the cubes of ice in your glass; not your children, who remained with their mother when you got a divorce and whom you never saw again; not even Alejandra, who died in an absurd accident.

His departure was something like an expulsion: upon finishing his drink, Juan Manuel quickly exited the putrid, filthy place.

Outside, he carefully scrutinized the statue of Saint George of Donatello, which stood in a niche in the front wall of the academy. He was still inspired enough to explain to Jimena the notable differences between the two hands of the warrior: the right hand, which was accustomed to brandishing a sword, was rough and virile; the left hand, which had held his shield, was delicate and feminine. Before the complacent look of the one who was capable of killing a dragon for the love of a damsel, he took Jimena's right hand and placed it against his, palm against palm, in order to prove his theory.

From there, he started down Moneda again and headed toward La Santísima Church, at which corner the street had changed its name to Emiliano Zapata. The buildings in that area had sunk considerably into the ground, and the pilaster base in the shape of truncated, inverted pyramids of the church's Churrigueresque façade was now covered with earth. Periodically, the doors had to be shortened in order to adapt them to the ever-growing height of the street. Searching for solutions, architects had decided to lower the depth of the ground in order to rescue the elegant lower proportions of the structure, because to accomplish the opposite, that is, to raise the church, would have been impossible. As a result, beginning at the academy, the street angled downward artificially, with periodic steps, until you reached the magnificent church, now proud to have been unearthed—recovered—to its original stature. Juan Manuel continued to explain the excavation process by pointing out the prominent steps that led downward to useless garage doors and by indicating the line on the buildings that marked the part that had been underground before the restoration had begun. Unsteadily, he continued walking along the street, interrupted periodically by steps that appeared haphazardly in his way, until he arrived at that last step in front of the Church of the Holy Trinity.

Despite the fact that his eyes were well trained to observe every detail of the architecture of the colonial period, he was always fascinated anew with baroque art and its purposes. Juan Manuel contemplated the large medallion in the center of the upper part of the façade, which represented the Holy Trinity, after which the church was named. One could barely see the dove representing the Holy Ghost that was perched on the stone cape draped over the Father's shoulders. It could well have been a clasp, not unlike the one on the Son's silklike cape, which is to say, in reality, the scene was the Holy Duality, he thought, with heretical joy. The Father and the Son. However, the Son wasn't nailed to the cross or held by the Father Almighty, as in other iconographic representations. No, the Son was lying across the Father's lap, as in so many other representations when he's on the mother's lap. A masculine Pietà, it was the omnipotent father lovingly holding his son in his lap.

Although he smelled of insomnia, nicotine, false teeth, and ear-wax, you were always laughing, Juan Manuel, like the times you would play horsey on his father's knees. He would lift his knees at the same time he imitated the clickety-clack of the horse's hooves.

Remember me, you who lost your memory and died without recognizing me . . . without knowing who the hell I was. Remember me. Let's play horsey, even if the stiff hairs of your three-day-old beard stick my cheeks, even if your hepatitis-laden breath asphyxiates me.

Suddenly, as if the memory of one to whom he owed his existence simply vanished into thin air, as if someone had cut the strings of the marionette, as if the Tres Coronas sherry, four beers, three tequilas, half bottle of wine, four brandies, two martinis, and two glasses of scotch had concentrated their effects at this particular moment, halfway down the steps that led to the church, Juan Manuel tumbled to the ground directly in front of the pained Father and dead Son.

CHAPTER 8

AFTER THE SECOND fall, he finally got his second wind. Juan Manuel stood up quickly and started walking like a body whose head had been lopped off by a guillotine.

Like some adventurous tourist wanting to get lost in an unknown city and take all the risks, he wandered aimlessly around the Merced area.

For instance, he walked down the street leading to the Plaza de la Alhóndiga, where dogs barked as loudly at night as the boom boxes blasted out music during the day. The place smelled like either stagnant water or leftover garbage from the market—spoiled vegetables, dead flowers, rotten fruit. Even if the establishments were closed, lighted signs on each side of the ever-narrowing street maintained vigilance over the fetid smells. Juan Manuel contributed to the stench of the street with a sporadic protean stream of urine. With arrhythmic steps he continued down the block and came to a plaza behind La Merced Convent.

That large solitary square, where years ago survivors of earthquakes would huddle together, had been converted into a gigantic garbage dump. After making his way through broken furniture and broken mirrors, empty picture frames, tricycles without wheels, and busted trophies, Juan Manuel finally inched his way to a window into which he could peer and marvel at the cloister of the convent.

The baroque and Mudéjar architecture had converted the stone into intricate lace and luxurious tapestries—bossed masonry, valances, draperies—all to Dr. Barrientos's continuing bewilderment and to the surprise of Jimena and Fernando. One by one, they grasped the iron grating over the window and peered inside at the prodigious spectacle.

Two street scavengers had just turned over some garbage cans at one corner of the plaza, which had become a staging area for garbage removal for La Merced neighborhood. They were sharing a beer and a cigarette while they sat on the edge of a fountain dedicated to Alonso García Bravo, an architect who had drawn the plans for the new colonial city by superimposing them over the pre-Colombian Mexico of Tenochtitlan. Curious yet greedy, they watched Juan Manuel present his soliloquy on baroque architecture with professorial expertise. Man, that guy is blitzed. They could have assaulted him and stolen his watch, wallet, pens, and gold-rimmed glasses, which were openly sticking out of the chest pocket of his blazer. They could have stripped him of his clothes—silk tie, wine-colored Italian loafers, argyle socks—and kicked the hell out of him. They could have left him naked in Alonso García Plaza, the plaza of la Merced, his plaza. But your hour hasn't arrived yet, Juan Manuel.

Dr. Barrientos continued through the deserted streets of La Merced. Without knowing how—the streets were so convoluted, and to top it off, he'd had a lot to drink—you come upon a dive that you've never been to before and whose name is unfamiliar to you.

A bouncer wearing a brown suit frisked you at the door. He ordered you to unbutton your jacket, he raised your arms, frisked you from your armpits to your ankles, and then waved you inside. Curiously, he didn't detect your monogrammed silver flask, which was in your back pocket. What an idiot! It could have been a pistol. You made an effort to look more or less sober, to try to walk straight and to articulate the few monosyllables necessary to buy a ticket that gave you the right to all the drinks you could handle and a seat in front of a stage.

The place is packed. Why, of course, it's Friday. Payday. There are bureaucrats, taxi drivers, bouncers with dark glasses and gold chains, and fat businessmen in festive groups at tables facing the stage in an oval on different levels. Without exception, everyone there is younger than you, Juan Manuel.

Wearing extremely high heels and scanty clothing and with protruding buttocks and pushed-up breasts looking like serving trays, women circulate endlessly among the tables like sluggish planets in orbit. Some are also seated with indecisive males waiting to make a transaction. Others dance on top of the tables among eager hands that reach up like the flames of purgatory, grasping for thighs and rear ends. Others give lap dances to innocent-looking guys who bought tickets to make out for the duration of a song. Is that a song? The multicolored glass reflectors that swivel to the rhythm of the music reveal the intense smoke of all the cigarettes in the world. The entire place smells of disguised sweat, industrial disinfectant, and cheap perfume.

You order a rum and Coke. Considering where you are, what else could you order? White rum. Given their accents and gesturing, to your right two Cubans—Senel and Arturo—you learn quickly that they're arguing to the point of no return. To your left, a young man sitting by himself is mesmerized by a female who attempts to dance gracefully to some music requiring sexual posturing. Holding your glass of rum with dirty ice cubes and fountain Coke, you observe the young, tawny, corpulent woman with blue eyelids and pearly lips who is decked out in a tiny skirt that reveals the bottom part of her butt and a striped blouse that barely covers her breasts. Sporting a pair of transparent plastic shoes, she struts around from one side of the stage to the other, taking larger steps than her legs would normally allow, while flouncing her voluminous thighs, which somehow fit with the size of her waist, and leaving in her wake as she walks past your covetous eyes the aroma of coconut oil, which ventilates your nostrils. When the music stops for a moment, the spotlights begin to blink off and on and point upward at a mirror ball over the stage that creates a twinkling effect against the black ceiling and walls. Next, an affected, almost unintelligible voice at the microphone makes a second call for the next stripper, Jessenia. She initiates her movements to an equally primitive music but even slower, or seemingly sensual. Sauntering, she starts to let down her black, abundant Aztec hair. She stares defiantly, even mechanically, at a crowd that, due to the spotlights, she probably can't even see. With a smirk on her face, she walks—dances?—from one side of the stage to the other side, which is opposite from where you're sitting, and swiftly unzips one side of her tiny skirt, which becomes a limp rag as she tosses it toward the stairs leading down to the audience. Once again, she struts across the stage, revealing her skintight red panties to a few guys who are hardly paying any attention to her. In another rapid movement, she removes her skimpy blouse and holds it against her chest for a few beats. Is this music measured by beats? Like a basketball star, she lands it next to what might be called her skirt, now exposing her drooping breasts and enlarged nipples. Mitigated somewhat by the high volume of the music, the noisy clamor of the crowd remains constant, despite the generous gestures of the dancer. The music begins to repeat itself. Accompanied by Jessenia, it continues inexorably. Now wearing only a pair of gold plastic earrings, the tiny red panties, and overly high heels, she walks over to the pole in the middle of the stage, which extends to the ceiling. Like a trained gymnast, she ascends the pole with agility. With her legs spread wide and her pubis caressing the chrome phallus, she makes a slow descent down the pole. Finally reaching the floor of the stage, she walks over to where you're seated and stops directly in front of you. Your eyes look straight at her calves. As she turns her back to you, you notice the cellulite invading her thighs and rear end. Ever so slowly, as if she were repenting, she begins to pull her panties down until, on one foot, she has to give them a clumsy jerk due to those extra-high heels. Then she tosses the panties into what looks like a dirty-clothes basket. A spotlight focuses on her pubic hair, which is shaved in a narrow stripe. Completely naked except for the earrings and high heels, she bends over, flexes her knees, spreads her legs as wide as she can, and shows you—only you—straight out, the lure and the disaster of her vagina.

"Move back, buddy," vociferates Senel, "because if that black lady farts, she'll knock your teeth out."

After a few coital movements, Jessenia sits up and squats in front of you. Her vagina is at eye level, only inches from your nose, allowing you to look into and even smell her body fluids, when she takes your head into her hands and pulls it in between her legs. As the disk jockey thanks Jessenia over the loudspeaker, she's already making her way toward the stairs leading down to the audience, where she discreetly picks up her clothes and disappears. Then the first call for Mayra is announced. She appears from the side of the stage, wearing a nurse's uniform with the typical Red Cross hat on top of her platinum-streaked hair, white apron, and white platform shoes that make her walk clumsily.

With hardly any variation, the same spectacle repeats itself. Her muscles, as well as her nipples, may be bigger; similarly, her skin and hair may be a different color, too, just like her pubic hair. Nevertheless, the ritual—the mechanical rhythm of the music, the length of the presentation, and the scanty clothes—is no different from the previous one.

As Mayra unties the bow of her apron and lets the strings dangle over her naked rear end, you become aroused by her puffy, pouting lips. You try to etch that image—her puffy lips, her hands untying the apron in the back, the shadow of the strings on her rear end—in order to try to re-create it sometime when you're alone. However, you know very well that when you need it, you won't be able to conjure up anything. You won't be able to retrieve it from your mental archive in which at this moment you're trying to store it. It's like an empty filing box.

On the other side of the stage, a large television screen projects two nude white women washing a sports car with a hose.

Young waitresses pass by without noticing you, or at least without showing that they're looking at you—at your age, at your tweed sport coat, and more important, your wallet bulging from your vest pocket. They walk around not looking at anyone, but wanting to be looked at. Appearing distant, inattentive, frowning, and wearing gaudy, cheap clothes and costume jewelry, they seem to be running errands.

First call for Berenice.

They want to be stared at, they want you stare at them, but they're not in charge of the transactions. Their job is to slink provocatively through the labyrinth of tables full of people, attract attention, show off their rear ends and breasts, and occasionally sit down next to some man. The women in charge are those wearing uniforms and tennis shoes and selling the tickets. With a ticket, a girl will dance for you, that is, she sits on your lap for the duration of one song. In front of everyone sitting around you, she rubs her body hard against yours. You can touch her anywhere except her genitals, which are covered with a G-string. If you want to take off her G-string, you have to buy three tickets and go to a small private cubicle covered by a curtain in front of which stands a bouncer.

Second call for Berenice.

· · · · ·

"To make you a man," your father had said at the end of his life.

He was tired of being a father. At that moment, amid the silence of his deafness, a hearing aid stuck in his ear, that transparent gaze always focused on the horizon, and a three-day-old stubble on his face, he had proposed a surrogate father for you for when you finished high school. It was Ángel, his first son, your half-brother, who was twenty years older than you, a person you barely knew.

"To make you a man," repeated your mother months later with that brooding voice barely into widowhood, when you finished

junior high. And, as a result, one night in early November she put
you on a bus that in a day would take you some 430 miles north
of Mexico City to Matehuala, San Luis Potosí, where, at barely fifteen years of age and under the tutelage of your half-brother, you
would become a man.

What did it mean to you then, Juan Manuel? To become a man?
To travel on a bus at night from the capital to Matehuala and to
recognize that small town where on the outskirts the passengers
would see a golden plaster key stuck to a pointed arch, which was
the only way, your mother had said, to know that you had arrived,
so as not to continue on to Saltillo. For you, to be a man meant
being able to read, without fear of reprisal, *La sangre devota* [*The
Devout Blood*], by Ramón López Velarde, the book—trembling like
a dove in your excited hands—that had found its way into your
heart and your memory ever since you bought it by saving your
allowance for seven weeks.

In the bus driver's rearview mirror, you could see the face of
a man—your face—surrounded by the smoke of a cigarette that
you dared to light after the man sitting next to you went to sleep.
It was the face of a freshly cracked nut sitting atop your neck, jaws
shut tight, and a faint shadow between your nose and mouth that
is commonly known as peach fuzz.

With only a dim light from above that hardly illuminated the
pages of your book, you felt something not unlike sadness in the
semidarkness of that bus. As you were getting on the bus, Mom
quickly gave you the sign of the cross, and as if you had become a
man, she said you would see each other at Christmas time. Suddenly, you were invaded by a smell of red wine, cooked apples, and
roasted pine nuts and hazelnuts. A lump rose in your throat that
your new manhood couldn't stop. Men don't cry, and you had to
face being orphaned for two months before the holidays.

The sun was just beginning to peek through the darkness in the
bus when you arrived at Matehuala. To your consternation, your
half-brother, Ángel, wasn't at the bus stop like your mother had
promised. You didn't recognize anyone amid the hustle and bustle

of straw hats. By the time all of the passengers had dispersed toward enviably known destinations, which made you envious, you cheeks were already burning. From behind, you felt a hand on your shoulder and a voice offering to take you to Don Ángel's house. At first, you thought he had been sent by your brother to pick you up, but then you realized that he was just a taxi driver who had detected a resemblance between you and "the boss."

"Ah, ha. You've got those same glassy eyes just like him," he said.

You arrived at your brother's house just as breakfast was being served. Ángel gave you an affectionate but overly strong pat on the head, like lowering the boom, that at least made it unnecessary to give him the customary kiss.

Since you had spent a sleepless night enveloped in the nomadic sadness of your regrettable travels, you thought you might be able to catch some shuteye during the morning before you had to become a man, which meant slowly getting settled into the guest room they had assigned to you. However, when you had barely finished eating a couple of scrambled eggs, Ángel took you to work at his store, La Central, located next to the town market, in his brand-new Chevrolet.

La Central was not what you expected. According to the way your father had described it to you one day, you imagined it to be something as extravagant as the Puerto de Liverpool department store in Mexico City, which is where you would go with your mother to buy things that you purchase only once in your life, such as pressure cookers, television sets, or Adela's First Communion dress. Instead, La Central was a dreary, small-town store next to the market. Although it was big, it was plain—no showcase windows or mannequins—only straw hats, blankets, pants, and shirts piled together next to bolts of decorative cloth in formation like soldiers standing at attention. Although your brother would attend to the countryfolk who had come to town from the surrounding villages, basically the store dealt mainly in wholesale goods that circulated far and wide, like some Mohammedan miracle, thanks to trucks that would haul away thousands of yards of batiste and poplin and hundreds of boxes of spools of thread that children would use to bury dead birds once they were empty.

You'll never forget that first morning working at La Central. As you were straightening up hundreds of straw hats, you could sense that the employees to whom you had not been introduced were watching you. They watched your every move, smiled with their eyes, and then chuckled without ever taking their eyes off of you. Despite that nut appearing atop your neck, that initial growth over your upper lip, and almost achieving the height of an adult, what were they looking at, Juan Manuel, if you still hadn't become a man?

When the female employees' giggling turned to questions, Ángel sent you to work with the men in the storeroom, where you were able to greatly expand your repertoire of obscenities.

At first, you were excited about working there, mainly because you wanted to show Chui, Germán, and Don Lupe that you were not some privileged spy for the boss. You learned how to remove the metal straps from boxes of clothing, to place blankets way up on the top shelves, to organize shirts by size, and to verify the dimensions of bolts of cloth. It wasn't long, however, before you learned to work with less zeal, given that your work habits had begun to stand out against those of your cohorts, all of whom would rest after opening each box, or eat quesadillas and smoke cigarettes mid-morning in that storage area where it was specifically prohibited to eat or smoke.

And even today, you still feel a heavy weight on your shoulders, mainly on your right shoulder, as if you were still carrying those bolts of cloth over to Chalita's store. Ángel had an urgent order to fill, so he took you from the storeroom to carry the bolts to her store a few blocks away. With difficulty, you swung three bolts of batiste onto your shoulder, and when you were about to leave on your first delivery, Ángel put a fourth package on top—in order to make you a man. You hadn't walked more than half a block when you began to feel the bolts of cloth slipping off your shoulder. The tips of your fingers barely sustained them. Like a stubborn mule, you calculated

that there were 115 steps left in order to reach Chalita's store, so you
started counting backwards . . . 115, 114, 113 . . . you can do it, I think
I can, I think I can, only 96 more to go . . . you can do it . . . 80, 79,
78 . . . until you finally arrived with only 14 steps left. No matter,
because as soon as you entered the store, the bolts of cloth slipped
from your shoulder and fell onto the dirty floor. Since the paper the
bolts were wrapped in was torn, the bolts of cloth unrolled along
the floor like a welcoming carpet, revealing amid Chalita's furious
gaze, the cloth's brilliant, multicolored prints. You couldn't keep
from laughing. How appalling was that? It took over your entire
body—your face, throat, lungs, belly, and shoulders. And your soul
as well. That was the last laugh of your adolescence.

Eight o'clock. You were always desperate for eight o'clock to roll
around and stop working. But why? There was nothing to do at
Ángel's house, where night after night the same domestic rituals were
repeated—scolding their children, your nieces and nephews, having
the same light meal, and saying good night and see you tomorrow
over and over again. Only *La sangre devota* waited intimately in your
room, along with an immeasurable longing to cry.

One afternoon, Ángel burst into the store and caught you on
top of one of the work tables reciting López Velarde's "La suave
patria" to the employees, who were fascinated, yet scoffed at you.
Although Ángel didn't say anything to you at the time, he looked at
you in bewilderment and then barged out of the store in the same
way he had entered. However, on the way home in the Chevrolet,
he said: "Before you came to Matehuala, the employees were real
dumb fucks," and just when you began to imagine that praise was
forthcoming in reference to your excellent relationship with Chui,
Germán, and Don Lupe, who, thanks to poetry, had adopted a better work ethic, you heard the crushing conclusion to his sentence,
"but ever since you've been here, they're even worse dumb fucks."

Workdays were long, way too long. Your hours expanded like
pulling on a wad of bubble gum. The hands of the clock moved
with sluggish annoyance. However, days off were even longer and
more boring. During the week, you anxiously awaited Sunday, and

on Sunday you longed for Monday in order to go back to work with Chui, Germán, and Don Lupe, who were your only friends . . . so far from home and so far from your mother.

On Sundays you would go to Mass with your brother, his wife, and their children. Since there was always one beautiful face that would appear at Mass in Matehuala, you would avidly and smugly entertain yourself with the novelty of examining the napes of the necks of those provincial girls, who, when you saw them from the front as they were leaving, had round, apple-shaped faces. As opposed to the meals during the week, you would always try to draw out those Sunday meals, because they were always preceded with a carefully measured aperitif—oh, how you wanted to have more than just sherry, you remember, like now, sitting here in this miserable dive, another rum and Coke, please, make it nice and strong, eh—which was always followed by a game of checkers that Ángel would propose threateningly and always win.

"You play like a woman," he used to say. "You make stupid moves."

Those afternoons were oppressive, and you missed your mother more than ever.

There was a run-down, decaying motel across the street from Ángel's house. It was falling down from disuse, now the victim of a recent surge of large, modern motels appearing along the highway on the outskirts of town. Matehuala, as it turns out, was the only place where a traveler could eat or spend the night between San Luis Potosí and Saltillo or Monterrey, which were 125 miles to the south and north, respectively. Matehuala was just a tiny dot on the map where you could return to the real world after having been lost in mirages created by the straight line of the highway from which there was nothing to see but a flat horizon interrupted by the odd cactus here and there and, from time to time, human phantoms selling iguanas and snakes.

Motel Prince was run by its owner—an aging, introverted gringo—who looked as bad off as the motel. Encapsulated in your memory, you can still see him wearing those blue jeans that in those days were not called by their brand name and that Scottish plaid shirt that matched his face after the six or seven shots of booze that he would consume as he talked to himself in English, starting at five o'clock every afternoon. He would always walk barefoot on the tiles in the reception area of the motel, which comprised the front desk with a cash register, a small bar with a coffee pot, a refrigerator full of Cokes, and a few laminated tables and folding chairs. But would you want to remember Mr. Prince? He did nothing to deserve a place in your memory. The one you want to remember is the young girl who worked for Mr. Prince, but no matter how hard you try, about all you can muster up is that frank smile, revealing a whiteness that contrasted with her dark skin and deep, dark— very dark—black eyes, now only a damp, wet, soaking mirage in the suffocating desert heat. Your thirst had been quenched.

On Sundays, you would watch her from your brother's garage. She would sit in that round, plastic wicker chair on the front porch of the motel, wearing her Sunday best and—too terribly early in life—feeling as lonely as you did.

She also had Sundays off, so after Mass she would most likely walk around the town's main plaza, where there's a wall with inscriptions on it, and buy an ice cream cone at La Michoacana. In the afternoons, she would return to the motel. She didn't have any friends in Matehuala, probably because she was from a nearby ranch. Instead of going inside to the reception desk or to her room at the back of the motel, she would sit bored, waiting, like you, for Monday to come around again. All the while, the plastic wicker chair would leave imprints on the backs of her bare legs.

Every Sunday you watched her through the iron grating that imprisoned you on your brother's property. Then you peeked at her through the thick hedge, but you never once dared to cross the street and talk to her. Why not, Juan Manuel? Because, instead of crossing the street and talking to her, you were trapped by the tribulations of only thinking about crossing the street and talking to her. You needed to conjure up something to talk about, like the times you would recite "La suave patria" in front of the bathroom mirror. You were simply unable to go over and sit down beside her. First, you had to think about it. Paralyzed, you were unable to let your pounding heart—similar to the intense buildup that you had been feeling in your genitals during the first fifteen years of your life—be your guide.

On one of those typically monotonous afternoons, Ángel took you with him to visit Mr. Prince. While your sudden eagerness made you blush, you recognized in your brother the real angel that was to lead you across the street. With your brother along, things would be a lot easier, and even if you didn't manage to strike up a conversation with her, at least you could say hello with the hope that maybe next week something might develop. However, making things easier like that frightened you even more; in reality, you preferred to give up and remain behind bars forever.

You crossed that wide median separating you from that girl, whose knees, given the way she was sitting in the chair, stood out like two protuberances from the geography of her body. She was seated next to two other chairs similar to hers. Instead of inquiring about Mr. Prince, as you thought he would do, Ángel sat down in the chair next to hers. You had no other choice but to sit down in the other chair. Ángel examined her body with ardor. Her name was Chabela. Raising ever so slightly the edge of her dress with his thumb and index finger and touching her thigh, he blurted out categorically:

"Poplin," he said.

Then he asked you: "Let's see what you've learned at La Central. In what width does poplin come?"

Of course, you didn't know what to say. You were ashamed of your brother, even though Chabela didn't seem offended. Her sadness quickly turned to laughter, and she even seemed happy. Even though you disapproved of what Ángel had done, you also got excited when he revealed her pretty legs, which you had longed to scale. Yet you despised him, because his vulgarity had shredded López Velarde's poetry, which you had hoped to recite to her when and if you ever got to be alone with her. Out of the blue, Ángel asked about Mr.

Prince, pointing to the door with his chin. She said he was probably having his first drink of the day.

"I'm going inside to see him," said Ángel, clumsily getting out of the chair into which he had almost disappeared. "I'm letting you take charge of Chabela," he said to you, winking his eye. "And watch out, eh, because she's mine. Right, Chabela?"

When Chabela giggled, you felt hurt.

Ángel went inside. You remained on the porch, staring at the marks on the backs of Chabela's legs from the plastic ribbing of the chairs. You just sat there with that idiotic smile on your face. In your head were those poems that now weren't worth a damn.

For a brief moment, you thought that you could imitate his words and laughter, which for better or worse had caused Chabela to laugh, but the feeling of revulsion had left you unable to utter a word, those terrifying syllables that cross our lips, meaning nothing. At the time, you didn't realize that it was precisely your silence that revealed how much you were taken by Chabela's black, very black, eyes, strong teeth, dark skin, and, above all, knees that protruded from that wicker chair, so very near your hand, Juan Manuel.

That's a bold move. Where did you get the nerve to put your hand on her knee? Especially you, who is so timid, humble, innocent. You couldn't believe it yourself. Who knows what invisible gods, so different and contrary to the other God in whom you once believed and loved, moved your right hand and deposited it on Chabela's protruding left knee, as if you were a checkers piece being moved by some superior force.

As if your hand were not resting on her knee, and with amazing naturalness, Chabela asked if you wanted to see her room, which was at the end of a row of small cabins. You nodded yes with that same look of idiocy and acquiescence while, at the same time, you clumsily tried to get out of that wicker chair, without knowing how to hide the tumultuous expansion in your trousers.

Her room was part motel room and part maid's quarters. It had a double bed with a red satinlike blanket, a minuscule bed lamp with a 25-watt bulb, a spacious but dilapidated bathroom that you could see from the front door, a chrome Sacred Heart of Jesus, a laminated green suitcase, an ironing board, some faded photos stuck into the mirror frame of a dressing table that was covered with jars of perfumed creams.

Chabela sat down on the stool in front of her dressing table and began to brush her black, lank hair. You just stood next to her, of course, knowing neither what to do nor what to say. Saying nothing herself, she just kept on brushing her hair, pretending not to see you in the mirror. Fearing she might be watching you anyway, you dared not look at her body. Why? You had already put your hand on her knee and managed to squint at her full, rounded buttocks, slanting upward at her waist. When she spoke finally, you let out a sigh of relief:

"Do you want to brush my hair?"

And who would believe it, Juan Manuel? You began to brush her hair. You brushed it with that typical virile awkwardness that caused her to squeal repeatedly, although the caresses of your left hand immediately quieted her from the brush strokes that rode roughshod over her head. Unexpectedly, you saw yourselves staring at each other reflected in the flaking, dull mirror, and you maintained the look an instant longer than if you had been looking directly at each other. After she squealed even louder and you said sorry, you sat down next to her on the stool, facing away from her. In the second it took for her to turn to you, she kissed you. At first, you didn't dare open your lips, not even your eyes. Next, however, like a fire leaping from an oven, you felt the surprising pleasure of her tongue sliding past your teeth into your mouth.

> Before your lips are gone forever,
> as I mourn, give them—
> perfume, bread, poison, a cure—
> to me at the definitive entrance
> to the cemetery.

Looking like she had been poured into those black leather pants, Berenice dances away happily with a smile that is contrary to her occupation, looking very professional. With her knees locked together, she shakes her buttocks just like the former black slave Antillean rumba dancers, who, they say, could move only that part of their anatomy because their ankles were shackled and they couldn't move around. As she removes her bra and twirls it like a cowboy lasso, the crowd reawakens and begins to cheer. Their enthusiasm isn't due to the generosity of her exposed breasts, which are truly massive yet firm, but to her laughter while she swivels her hips and captures the imagination of those who are watching. During her second call, and with unflinching satisfaction, she unzips her leather pants from waist to ankle and unleashes in all of her nudity the fullness of her rear end, which almost brings down the house. Berenice finishes her number and picks up the remnants of what had previously covered her nudity. Juan Manuel has become distracted, while in the background the music cranks up again, almost drowning out the shrill voice announcing the arrival of Tamara, who prances out onto the stage with boots that reach halfway up her thighs. May she never take them off, he prays.

· · · · ·

By the time you left Chabela's room, it was dark outside. Mr. Prince had left the reception desk, and your brother had left, too. He would be at home.

You looked over the route back and crossed the avenue unnoticed. You didn't have keys to get in, so you got worried that Ángel might be upset that you were coming back so late, and he'd be even more irritated if you rang the doorbell and woke him up. You considered going back to Chabela's room and spending the rest of the night there, just as she had asked you to do—stay with me—and surround yourself with the aroma of her shoulders and the freshness of her arms. But you also figured that your brother would be extremely put out if you didn't go home. As you approached the gate, you could see a light in the living room. I'm going to knock, you thought. If they open the door, I'll take the scolding and be done with it. If they don't open up, I'll go back to Chabela's room. You knocked once, so as not to wake up Ángel if he was already asleep, and that way you could tell him in the morning that no one came to the door. I hope no one comes. You wanted to retrace your steps and return to that eager tongue and those pretty knees that had separated to allow you access to that humid, warm, pinkish world that you had never experienced before and into which you had entered precipitously. You counted the seconds from the time you knocked on the door—one, two, three. If by the time I reach sixty—one minute—I'm going back. Thirty-two, thirty-three, thirty-four. At forty-seven, Ángel opened the door. He looked serious, but he wasn't mad. As you went into the house, you said goodbye to that night forever. And your brother said the worst thing he could have ever said at that moment:

"Let's play a game of checkers."

You wanted to go to bed and embrace your desire for Chabela, lick your sore lips, relive the debut of your genitals, but okay, if you want to, I'll take red.

Drowsy, you sat down in front of Ángel at the kitchen table. He had always won without much difficulty, because it was too much work for you to anticipate every single move. Your intuition is better than your logic, but this time something extraordinary happened. Despite your sleepiness, the distraction caused by Chabela's perfume, which drenched your body, and the slight twinge of discomfort that gave existence to your testicles, you beat him. You beat Ángel—your brother, your boss, your surrogate father. You beat him for the first time since arriving at Matehuala. For the first time in your life. And you couldn't believe it.

Now, finally, you could not only go to sleep, but also initiate that heroically insane habit of talking to yourself alone. But, no, Ángel wanted a chance to get even. There was no way to say no to him, so it was another game using the same color—red. And you beat him—the one who considered himself to be Chabela's owner—for the second time.

"Okay, let's go to bed now. This is not my day," he said, giving you a strong but affectionate pat on the cheek.

And now, Juan Manuel, as Tamara dances in front of you, you finally understand. You're on the verge of crying, and you want to hug and thank him. Forty years later, you finally understand. You're a jerk not to have realized that in order to make you a man that Sunday, your brother Ángel had to let you win all the games.

CHAPTER 9

D R. BARRIENTOS followed his Stations of the Cross. He had decided to leave in a leisurely fashion. He didn't have to tell anyone, because there was no need to pay a bill upon leaving. Here, the drinks were always paid for up front.

Although it was difficult, he stood up firmly from his chair. His attempt to leave was thwarted by the Exterminating Angel, who offered him another drink.

"The same, sir?"

"Yes, please," he stuttered.

He took advantage of being upright to go to the bathroom while they brought him another rum and Coke. Following the directions the waiter gave him, he entered a maze of dark hallways that led to some steep stairs reminiscent of a Mesoamerican pyramid. At one point, he saw several seminude women humping half-dressed men. The force of their movements indicated that they had gone beyond erotic play to the work of sex. For them, eroticism was the same as a job.

It was semirigid, but not quite stiff, so urinating was somewhat difficult. Brushing aside the aggressive restroom attendant who was selling paper towels, chewing gum, antacids, and condoms, he exited the restroom, only to witness again from above a scene of condemnation—public copulation. On the stage below, Pamela performed daring movements with her pronounced jaw and protruding buttocks that paralleled the other women's movements. Dozens of women were straddling men sitting in their chairs. You could barely hear the music over the spontaneous, brutal, and boisterous laughter of the machos and the fake, almost intelligent panting of the females. Rotating reflectors revealed waists, zippers, high heels, nipples, saliva, anuses, fallen socks, sweat, glasses, earrings, and thick body hair.

Amid that artificial underbrush that somehow seemed to cover the women's nudity, Juan Manuel saw—as if she were a fleeting apparition—a young girl dressed in white. Her tiny dress barely covered her body, and she was wearing a gold chain around her right ankle. Grasping the handrail of the stairs on the second floor, he followed her with inflamed eyes until some jerk behind him brought him back to reality—keep moving, keep moving.

Wanting to chase after that apparition, he stumbled and almost fell down the entire staircase. Once he reached the ground floor, he searched anxiously for his drink. You don't remember that you had already finished your last drink and had ordered another one, but the server hadn't brought it because you weren't there. Of course you didn't find it, so you ordered another one from the first person who passed, but the guy wasn't a waiter, and he almost took a swing at you, who do you think I am, you jerk. You wandered abstemiously around the bar area, looking for a drink, a place to reside, and little Fuensanta, Ramón López Velarde's first love and poetic muse. At last you saw her go by. She was pulling along some bewildered-looking young man, as if he were a dog. Then they disappeared into that dark labyrinth. Once again, and in vain, he looked around for his seat and his drink. He finally found another spot, right next to the hallway down which Fuensanta had escaped with her dog. They brought him his first drink.

You patiently await Fuensanta's liberation and take a few sips of your rum and Coke. Your right cheek starts twitching; it stops, and in a few seconds, your nose starts twitching, then your forehead. You see next to you the repeated tired image of a woman dissolving into the opening of a large shell. Her toes are swollen and choked by the straps of her high heels. They look like kernels of corn on a cob. She can't really handle those heels. You try to imagine her when she was young or, better yet, the moment when she wakes up every morning, but you immediately reject any feelings of compassion or any thoughts on the immorality of the situation.

The mirrors multiply a dancer's movements. Gladys? Ninfa? Zulema? Her reflection arouses you more than looking directly at her.

A woman dressed in a uniform with a short skirt and tennis shoes approaches to sell you a ticket. You're unable to speak clearly, you can't roll your R's, your mouth is dry, you're suffocating, you need something wet. Despite all that, you manage to inquire about how the game works and then you decide to participate. If you buy a ticket, you can choose any woman—all of whom are practically naked—to dance for you right where you're sitting. You can touch any part of her except the genitals. And if you purchase three tickets, you can go with her to a private room, where she'll dance three songs, just for you, but completely naked this time. Songs? Yes, three musical numbers. Musical? Imprudently, you pull out your wallet. You purchase three tickets. Stuttering with a stupid smile on your face, you request Fuensanta.

"Who?"

"Fuensanta . . . the little girl . . . white dress . . . gold anklet. She left with a dog."

"What do you mean, a dog?"

"No, a man, a young man."

"I don't know who you're talking about, but I'll try to find her for you."

You have three tickets in your hand. The twitching starts again, in your right cheek, your nose, your forehead, and then your cheek, your cheek, your cheek. On stage, Gladys-Ninfa-Zulema is naked with a ring hanging from her vagina.

They're like prey, you thought. Chastised. Forced. This place is a jail. Then you decide to change the topic so as not to dampen your eagerness for Fuensanta, who will appear at your table and sit down beside you at any moment. There are just three tickets between you and her. Where will she put the tickets? In which part of her scanty clothing?

Sitting next to you is a group of rough-looking soldier-types, who are drinking and singing in chorus fashion. With a high-class air, two near-naked strippers are sitting with them., They crook their little fingers when they lift their glasses to drink. When they laugh, they cover their mouths with the palms of their hands. When they wiggle, they try to keep tiny pieces of cloth in place over their genitals. Despite the loud music, you hear—you think you hear—a police raid. When it happens, there's no problem. Over there, the strippers' fingers and orange nail polish are pointing upward and away from their glasses. You're clutching your tickets. The veins in your hand. Your twitching cheek. The glass. Rum and Coke. A police raid. Heart throbbing in your testicles. Tiny pieces of cloth tied around her waist. The little finger. Orange nail polish. Vaginal ring. The rhythm of the music. The spotlight. The mirror. Rum and Coke. Vibration. The operative. The fingernail. Bass guitar. Your testicles. Fuensanta.

Accompanied by the uniformed lady with the short skirt and tennis shoes, Fuensanta finally appears at your table.

"Is this her?"

"Yes, it's her."

White dress. Anklet. Black hair. They leave her with you. After she greets you with a shrill voice and a tired smile, she kisses you on the cheek. She sits down next to you. Hi, you say to her, but nothing else. What else is there to say to her? She's a dark-complexioned, well-developed young woman—but almost a child. She smiles at you like a professional. You observe her bare thighs near your hand, and a god much different from the one you used to believe in places your hand on her leg. Without flinching, she only smiles.

"What's your name, Fuensanta?"

"Fuen . . . what?"

"No matter. What's your name?"

"Glafira. And yours?"

And what is your name, Juan Manuel?

"Ramón," you respond, "Ramón Lopez."

Seemingly indifferent to your presence or distracted by the music, she calculates how long she'll need to take you to the private room and comply with the rules of the three tickets. She doesn't pay any attention to you until it's time to go. With her humiliating youth radiating outward, she suddenly stands up and takes you by the hand. And you, concealing an inflamed liver, can barely stand up. Before giving her your hand and allowing her to lead you through the maze of tables, like a dog on a leash, her arm, you snatch your drink from the table and follow her toward the small private room with a curtain in front, next to which the chimpanzee waits to take your tickets. After having to wait a few more seconds for the music to finish, the chimpanzee opens the curtain and a half-naked woman leaves, followed by a man who looks completely dazed. You encounter the only pieces of furniture—a small stool in front of an armchair covered with imitation leather—in the tiny room barely large enough for two people, if one is on top of the other. After Fuensanta goes in, she orders you to sit down and wait until the next song starts. You obey. You set your rum and Coke on the floor next to your chair.

With the blink of an eye, at the same time that an electronic voice in the bar announces Mildred's heated entrance, Fuensanta takes her clothes off. Before you can revel in the image of her body barely covered by those tiny bits of cloth, she has removed them with professional aplomb. During the first song, she dances completely naked in front of you. She stands on the stool. Gyrating, she caresses her breasts and genitals. As the first part finishes, that is, the first ticket, she turns her back to you. While she bends over and exposes her intimate parts, she smiles back at you from under her legs, now the symbols of her spoils. Drooling, you can only stare stupidly back at her. Meanwhile, her long hair dangles onto the pestilent carpeting.

During the second song, she removes your tweed blazer, loosens your silk tie, unbuttons your shirt, shamelessly places her hand on your crotch, and with military dexterity tries to bring your virile member to attention, even though—like you—it remains at ease. Then she places her thighs on your chest and starts to lower them slowly, rubbing them hard against your bare belly, down to your drunken member, which you scrubbed so diligently that morning, knowing—or hoping—that you would use it for the last time. She's moving between your legs, she naked, you dressed but without coat and with loosened tie, unbuttoned shirt, gray chest hairs exposed and paunch spilling over your belt. You caress her youthful arms and shoulders. Since she can't see you, you dare to squeeze her voluptuous breasts. She's a compassionate woman, because she gives you—gives you?—permission to run your hands all over her firm body while at the same time electric impulses throb in your cheeks and the triglycerides in your blood turn your face red. You're want to retain that tactile image in your hands. You want her breasts and thighs to transform your fingerprints, your signature, your portrait, and your credentials. Ultimately, you want the second song to last forever.

During the third song, she kneels down in front of you and begins rubbing your member with her hand through your pants. She doesn't caress it, no, she rubs it hard, and it begins to hurt more than feel good. Suddenly, not knowing why, maybe because you were so happy, you become frustrated, because you don't know what the hell you're doing there. You want the song to be over quickly. Where does she think this will take you? You're neither going to be able to ejaculate there, nor will you go somewhere else with Fuensanta to do it. And even if you did take her somewhere else, you wouldn't be able to do anything with her, because you're filthy drunk, Juan Manuel. So, you become impatient.

"Stop, stop," you say.

Grasping her wrist, you push away the hand that's mechanically going up and down. You want to take a sip of your rum and Coke that's on the floor next to you.

"What's wrong, Gramps? You don't like it?"

The word "Gramps" erupts like a migraine headache. You don't even bother to answer her politely: No, it's not that, it's just . . . You shake your head. If you could see yourself now. Completely flushed, your eyelids are so swollen that only a narrow band of your eyes can be detected. You can't even talk. Sweat runs down your temples. Your hair is disheveled.

Saved by the bell. As the third song comes to an end, three claps are heard at the entrance to that fetid cubbyhole. Fuensanta picks up the tiny pile of clothes and puts them on as fast as she took them off. Before you're able to button your shirt, straighten your tie, and put on your blazer, the curtains open inopportunely and Glafira, without saying good-bye, bolts out.

The person who opened the curtain behind which Dr. Barrientos sat with his shirt unbuttoned, loose tie, and no sport coat was not the bouncer who had ushered him in three songs ago, but the operative.

Three policemen with machine guns pointing at the ceiling were standing where the curtain covered the front of that jail cell where Juan Manuel couldn't even fit lying down. Nervous, and clumsily trying to button his shirt, he looked up at them with bloodshot eyes and observed them from head to toe, from their field caps to their boots.

"Put all of your possessions on the stool," one of them commanded.

It was difficult for him to stand up. He unhooked the key chain from a belt loop on his jeans and put it on the small stool on top of which Fuensanta had danced naked. He took his red handkerchief—wrinkled but still clean—and some change from his pants pocket. He felt the pocket of his half-buttoned shirt and pulled out his parking stub and a Maalox tablet.

"This, too?" he asked.

"Are you deaf? I said everything."

He put them on the stool. One of the policemen grabbed the stub.

"What's your license plate number?" he commanded, as if he were conducting a drill.

Juan Manuel remembered. The number coincided with the one on the stub. Then he answered other questions. Isuzu. Metallic blue. 1996.

"Now the things in your jacket," he ordered.

Holding his tweed jacket with one hand, he started to remove its contents with the other. First out on the stool of the accused were his gold-framed glasses. Next, what a pity, he placed his pocket diary and pens on the stool of the accused. And, last but not least, he pulled out his wallet, which contained his driver's license, business cards, credit card charges, and bills of different denominations. Fortunately, he had left his credit cards at home.

"Is that it?"

"That's it," he answered, handing his jacket to them for their own verification. There wasn't anything else. One of them picked up the Montblanc pens and demanded an importation permit. You have to hide a laugh and just look at them stupidly.

"This is contraband," he said. "We'll have to confiscate them."

After flipping through your pocket diary, they tore out the page with your personal information, and the one who had kept the parking stub put the diary into his coat pocket.

"Your license has expired," he snapped.

They also confiscated his gold-rimmed glasses, keys, wallet, watch, everything.

"You don't have any credit cards?" they inquired.

"I don't use them. You never know when you're going to get mugged," he responded with some courage.

They threw his tweed jacket into his face.

"Get dressed, you son of a bitch. Just look at you. Aren't you embarrassed?"

They left.

Stripped of his possessions, Juan Manuel finished buttoning his shirt, straightening his tie, and putting on his sport coat. As he was starting to abandon the cubbyhole, he spied his hip flask—with his initials J.M.B.A.—in the armchair. He picked it up lovingly and stuck it back in his hip pocket. It had slid out while Fuensanta imposed her movements on him. He wasn't able to leave until the police, accompanied by several other women, left. Then he saw Fuensanta. She had changed clothes and was laughing as she hugged the same policeman who had taken his possessions.

· · · · ·

Stumbling, Dr. Barrientos walked in no particular direction along those deserted streets during the wee hours of the morning. He had undone his tie and wrapped it around his neck like a scarf. His shirttails hung out below his sport coat, covering his redemptive hip flask, which conformed perfectly to the shape of his right buttock.

He came upon La Soledad Church, which, during the Viceroyalty, was known as the thieves' church because, throughout the day, in that spacious atrium robbers sold what they had stolen the night before. The victims whose houses had been robbed could go there the next day and buy back their wives' jewels, silver candlesticks, porcelain dishes, and even horses, on the condition that, in order to stay alive, no one would claim ownership of the merchandise that had been stolen.

From the steps leading down to the atrium, he could size up the primitive dominion of the church, its deformity, and the gigantic proportions of the walls supporting the cupola. Faltering, he staggered down the steps and crossed the solitary atrium. Like a wounded bull that runs toward the barrier in a bullring, he made a beeline toward the façade of the church, where he caressed a small part of the base of a stone niche that enveloped a saint—now eroded, faceless, and without an identity. Taking the flask out of his back pocket, he unscrewed the lid and took a sip. He put the lid back on and discreetly placed the flask at the feet of the anonymous saint, directly behind the stone folds of his tunic, for him to look after it.

He leaned against the wall, facing the enormous plaza, and like drops of water dripping down a wall, he slid to the ground.

CHAPTER 10

A s he lay asleep propped up against the wall of La Soledad Church, two thieves went through his pockets. Since someone had beaten them to it, they found nothing—no wallet, no pens, no watch. Their only option, consequently, was to steal his clothes. Even though they were wrinkled and soiled, they still looked expensive. After they removed his silk tie, they flipped a coin to see who would get it. Then they took off his blazer and again flipped a coin to determine its new owner. They did the same with his shirt, his wine-colored loafers, his argyle socks, and his leather belt. However, they didn't remove his jeans, because they were old and tattered and had no value. Besides, he had urinated in them.

• • • • •

You're sitting on a bedpan next to your bed. You're a child but you have a body that is now tired and worn out. You're naked, with your underwear around your ankles. You're unable to lift your feet off of the cold ceramic tiles. You're cold. You count the tiles, and every time you get to twelve, you have to start over. The design is like your spinal column. You can see your vertebrae in them. From above, you see yourself down below, naked, sitting on the bedpan. The cold gives you goose bumps. Your mother gets up wrapped in a white sheet. She's not your mother, it's Violeta, your children's mother. She has dark circles around her eyes, as if she were wearing a mask, but they are her eyes. She's the mother of your children, Violeta, but she's also your mother. She tries to remove the sheet and put it around you, but she can't pull it off—her body is the sheet itself. She never manages to cover either your bare shoulders or the vertebrae protruding from your spinal column, which you can see from above, as if your eyes were on the ceiling. Seated on the bedpan while you count the twelve ceramic tiles over and over again, you wait for your mother, or Violeta, to cover your shoulders with the sheet. But it never happens. And you're so cold. And it's so cold around you. You feel like crying, but you can't. There are no tears. They're frozen in your eyes, like stones that hurt your eyelids. You gently rub them with your knuckles to make the pain go away. After a short while, the ice begins to melt, but still no visible tears. They remain inside you. In the darkness, however, you see some momentary flickering, but it doesn't take away the cold. It's too deep inside you. It's in your bones. You vigorously rub your upper arms with the palms of your hands. The flickering continues off in the distance in the silence of the night, sometimes in slow motion, other times like lightning. It's still nighttime, Juan Manuel. The gloomy, solitary streetlamps fail to illuminate the immensity of the area. Except for cars on the other side of the plaza, where you're sitting on the ground, practically naked, leaning against the wall of La Soledad Church, there's no sound.

While you were asleep, you were robbed again. This time, they took your clothes. Now you have no jacket or shirt. You're naked from the waist up. You try to put your arms around yourself and rub your shoulders. And you have no shoes. They even took your socks. You rub your freezing feet. Damn, it's cold. At least the thieves didn't harm you. When you run your fingers over your body, you get scared that you might find a knife wound; but they didn't hurt you, they just took your clothes. And you didn't even realize it. At least they left you with your jeans, but as you look down, they're soaked with urine. Compulsively, you search for your hip flask in your back pocket. It's gone. They stole it, too, you think. You try to sit up, but you can't. You're thirsty, really thirsty. Hoping to find your flask, you check your pockets again. You double-check, now sure that they took it, along with your sport coat, your shirt, and your shoes. Your thirst makes you stand up. Then you realize that they also took your belt. No matter, the jeans are tight enough not to fall down. Your belt isn't that important, anyway. But the flask is. You need it. Once you manage to stand up in front of the anonymous saint, you remember that you put it under his protection after taking a sip before your third fall. While the saint couldn't protect you from the thieves who stole your clothes, he did protect your blessed flask. There it is, hidden between the folds of his tunic. Trembling, you take it into your hands, remove the lid, take a swig that burns your throat, and then feel it warm your joints. You put it back into your hip pocket. Now you need that Maalox tablet. You thank the saint for the miracle and start off walking.

Where are you going, Juan Manuel? Now that you're barefoot, how are you going to walk through the garbage in the plaza in the dark? You'll destroy your feet. Where are you going? There's nothing left to steal, except for your silver flask . . . and your life.

To the main plaza. The very center of the city. The Zócalo.

Sidestepping puddles, rocks, and garbage while at the same time dodging broken glass, rusty nails, and excrement, Dr. Barrientos crossed through the courtyard of the thieves' church. Man, there's a lot of shit in this place. Going up the same steps that he had stumbled down, he found himself on a sidewalk next to the beltway that you don't remember having crossed earlier in the day.

At that hour—who knows what time it was by then—there still wasn't much traffic, only a few heavy trucks lumbering along with their goods on board, a few taxis, and the odd inebriated automobile barreling down the roadway at high speed, disobeying traffic lights. It frightened him to have to cross that wide roadway because he couldn't run, drunk and barefoot as he was. Moreover, he felt a little embarrassed to cross such a wide street—there was no place to hide. He just stood on the sidewalk, waiting for a chance to cross. A taxi stopped in front of him without Juan Manuel's flagging it down. The taxi driver, upon seeing him in that condition—half-dressed and barefoot, yet looking somewhat distinguished—most likely thought, correctly so, that he had been mugged or kidnapped, which could lead to a handsome tip by offering his services.

"Do you want a ride home, young man? If you like, you can pay me when we get there."

You consider the possibility of getting into the taxi and escaping this nightmare, returning home, resting, sleeping for three days, but you instantly reject the option. You have to go to the Zócalo, to the center of the center. Whether you want to admit it or not, that's the way it's written, damn it.

"That's the way it's written, damn it," you say to the taxi driver, who doesn't understand what you're saying, so he swears at you and accelerates rapidly, disappearing onto the beltway.

Once again, he waited to cross the roadway. When it was all clear, he ran as fast as his drunkenness and lack of shoes allowed. While he didn't stumble, his feet were starting to hurt. There were no cuts that were bleeding, no broken glass or rusty nails, but he had scraped the white, smooth bottoms enough that they were now black and rough. He sat down on the other sidewalk and began to rub them, noticing that they were throbbing to the point that it seemed like his heart was in his feet.

The smell of frying food distracted him from his self-applied physical therapy. On that side of the roadway, there was an all-night food stand where you could buy pork tacos. He hadn't eaten anything since leaving Bar Alfonso, which was some time ago, or to be exact, ever since he had purchased that bag of pumpkin seed wafers in Dulcería Celaya, just after leaving Bar Alfonso. He was hungry, and at the same time, he felt nauseous. He decided to try some meat tacos, as his friend Rubén says, the ones that are so fresh they still bark. And let's see if I can find a beer somewhere, too. He started walking toward the taco stand. As he approached, he suddenly remembered that he had been robbed of everything. He didn't have a cent to his name, nothing. Now he felt doubly naked, but there was no way he was going to utter those painful words— Hey, buddy, got some change for a taco—the same words that this same morning he had responded to in the negative to someone. He swallowed some saliva and stopped himself from opening his flask again. There's only one swallow left, Juan Manuel, so keep it for the end. So, he initiated his painful trek down Soledad toward the National Palace.

Since he only needed his glasses for reading, he managed to spot the severe, impregnable back door to the palace at the end of the street.

Practically naked and feeling the painful abrasions on the bottoms of his feet, he started out once again toward the main plaza by walking back down Soledad, flanked by metal shutters over store fronts, disintegrating balconies, and the voracious fangs of stray dogs.

By taking your pens, they also purged you of the annoying responsibility of writing and spending hour upon hour trying to fill a reluctant page, similar to that plate of green beans on the table in front of you when you were a little boy. Now you don't have to write every morning. What for? Everything has already been written. Your own life, your imminent death, a death from which not even your stupid writing can save you. You can't read either because they took your glasses. You can still see in the distance, but up close everything is hazy and distorted. Words in a book are now but diffuse stains without any meaning. You can neither read nor write. And you can't even go home. Since you don't have the keys to your house, now you don't have a house either. No house, no books, no records, no paintings, no bed, no desk, no toilet, no wine, no checkbook, no identification, no passport, no birth certificate, no diplomas, no money, and not even a car to drive around in, because with the parking stub and the information you gave them now in the hands of the police, your car, at this time of night . . . at what time, Juan Manuel? You don't even have a watch. What would happen if the sun never came up, if this night were to linger for all eternity? Since you don't have a watch, perhaps time has stopped tonight . . . maybe forever. Without a watch, time has ceased to exist. No appointments either, because they stole your pocket diary. You have no past, no future. You have no memory, no hope. All you have is one last swig from a silver flask with your initials—J.M.B.A.—on it. That's for the final hour.

Even though the bottoms of his feet were raw, Juan Manuel got to Correo Mayor, which led straight to the back door of the National Palace. He would have to go all the way around in order to reach the Zócalo on the other side of the plaza. He hesitated between going north down Moneda or south down Corregidora. He decided to take the longer route in order to avoid going back the same way he had come. He walked down the cobblestone street on the side of which there were gutters filled with stagnant water and detritus. Finally, he arrived at the garbage-strewn Zócalo. Nary a soul was there, not even the usual group of laborers on a hunger strike in front of the mayor's office. No one. From the corner of the Supreme Court of Justice Building, he could see the imposing, intrepid cathedral. He pointed himself in the direction of the flag-staff, which was without a flag at that hour. What time of night is it, Juan Manuel? He sat down at the base and hugged the gigantic pole just the way he imagined a captain would embrace the mast of his sinking ship.

CHAPTER 11

SCATTERED ACROSS the wide expanse of the Zócalo were the remains of a previously discarded day. Like any other day, there were mounds of garbage, the product of street vendors, more nomadic than even those who inhabited the surrounding streets, not to mention the thousands and thousands of pedestrians who, like members of an ant colony, had conglomerated there from early morning to late evening. The area reeked of burned charcoal from portable cooking stoves and of excrement.

There was no moon. The amber lights of the cathedral bell towers had been turned off hours before, and the silhouette of the steeples, closely guarded by warlike saints, could barely be distinguished from the dark sky. Like a mortal wound, located between the Metropolitan Chapel and the National Palace beyond Seminary Plaza, was the cavity of the Templo Mayor of ancient Tenochtitlan. San Ildefonso, now a dried scab, was hardly visible as well. The Royal Pontifical University of Mexico was nearby, too. Despite the yellowish color of its restoration, it seemed to exude the mournful color of the togas and airs of its ancestral inhabitants. The dome

of Santa Teresa seemed like the tower of a mosque in the middle
of a military encampment. Only a small, dreary light illuminated
the bell of Dolores above the presidential balcony of the National
Palace. There were no lights coming from the windows of the old
town hall buildings, which were artificially divided by Veinte de
Noviembre Avenue, also deserted at that hour of the night. Even
the Hotel Majestic was dark, and the tables at the bar on the terrace had been folded up like sleeping birds. Commercial establishments under the arched walkways—restaurants, boutiques, jewelry
stores—displayed nothing more than their locked metal shutters.
Traffic lights glowed uselessly in the dark, and the flying buttresses
illuminated nothing but the silence of the monstrous plaza. Everyone had disappeared—the dancers with their shells and drums, the
street hawkers with their wares, and the snake-oil sellers with their
words. And it was still too early for the orange-uniformed street
sweepers to remove the garbage, the newspaper sellers to open their
newsstands, or the military guard to raise the flag and render the
proper military honors. There was no one around, with the exception of a few beggars sleeping on the steps of the old town hall.
Only Juan Manuel Barrientos in the middle of the plaza, naked,
disheveled, and dirty at the base of the flagpole like a ghost.

All of a sudden, screaming voices rip through the silence between
the Metropolitan Chapel and the Templo Mayor. Some impetu-
ous shadows, seemingly seized with fear, rush out into the Zócalo.
Hesitating for a second or two, they look back and decide to make
a dash for the flagpole. They first follow the iron fencing in front of
the cathedral and then go through the porticoes along the sides of
the plaza, intending to cross the plaza diagonally and escape down
Dieciséis de Septiembre. Two men are fleeing from someone. Their
steps sound like horses' hooves at full gallop. They're stampeding like
hunted animals. They aim for the flagpole. Juan Manuel watches
them approach him. Additional steps, equally swift, are heard coming behind them, accompanied by their respective shadows, which
are screaming threats and improprieties. Now vulnerable as they
run across the open plaza, the two men who are fleeing neither

say anything nor look back. They keep running as fast as they can
. . . toward Juan Manuel, who can already hear their heavy panting. Hot in pursuit, one of the shadows stops, after which a shot
is heard, obliterating the silence. Just before reaching the flagpole,
one of the pursued falls to the ground. Juan Manuel sees his face at
the moment he's shot. The other one who's being pursued turns to
look at his companion, fallen on his back. Juan Manuel can see that
wide-eyed look on the other's face, whether to stay with his friend
or to continue running. He decides to keep running toward the
flagpole. Now he's close, very close to Juan Manuel. Now frightened
and confused, Juan Manuel stands up to watch the spectacle unfold.
Everything is happening too fast. There's no warning. More shots
are heard, but they miss their mark. The one who is still running
makes it to the flagpole and jumps up onto its base. He quickly
hides behind Juan Manuel and puts his arm around his neck. He
has a knife in his hand. Juan Manuel first sees the knife, which the
man places against his neck, then he recognizes the sleeve of his
tweed sport coat. Another shot rings out. The man loosens his grip
on Juan Manuel, who then falls down onto the base of the flagpole,
but not before hearing a last shot that brings down the assailant as
he takes off running.

CHAPTER 12

S PRAWLED OUT on the ground with your arms outstretched at the base, on your back, exposed to the four winds of the Zócalo, you feel cold again. You could have covered yourself with newspapers or cardboard boxes like the beggars under the porticoes, but who would have thought that someone was going to shoot you in the middle of the Zócalo? And you're not even a national hero, you bastard. The sticky dampness of your jeans chills your inner thighs. You feel your wet underwear. Given the humidity and cold, your testicles and your penis have shriveled. You want to unzip your pants, stick your hand inside your underwear, and rearrange your genitals, but you can't move. It's so cold your nipples get hard and the gray hair on your chest and arms sticks up. You're shivering all the way down to your feet, which swelled up because of the long walk. You can feel how they've become enlarged and flushed, now throbbing strongly. They seem as if they're going to explode, but they're freezing cold. Oh, how you'd like to stick them into a bucket of hot water, or take a bath perfumed with oily fragrances that would anoint your entire body, get into bed with soft, clean sheets, cover yourself with a down comforter, lay your head down on a warm, comfy pillow, and go to sleep . . . for three days, waking up for absolutely nothing. You feel something stuck in your back—perhaps tiny pieces of rock, debris, or glass. You feel the pressure of your silver flask on your right hip. You want to brush off whatever is stuck to your back, but you can't move. Your left arm is numb. You can't feel it. You try to open and close your left hand, but it's impossible. It remains half open, half closed. Your right hand responds normally, moving when you tell it to, but any movement, however insignificant, hurts. Part of your side and back feels wet, as if you had fallen into a puddle of water. When you flex your right hand, your heart hurts. Nevertheless, you raise your arm, cross it over your chest, and run it inch by inch over your left side in search of the source of the thick liquid dripping to the ground from your back. Your fingers discover a fleshy, jagged buttonhole that makes you scream from pain when you barely touch it. You put your arm back where it was, flat on the ground. That simple movement leaves you exhausted. It's hard to breath. It hurts each time you exhale. You breathe just enough to stay alive, Juan Manuel. Nothing more. In. Out. You can hear yourself breathe. In. Out. In. Out. You can hear your breathing, like sad moaning, bounce off the silence of the night. That's curious: you're cold, but you're sweating. You can feel beads of sweat run down your forehead, your temples, and your neck. In. Out. You're hungry, but you also feel nauseous. You want to throw up to get rid of all that alcohol that you've been ingesting all day and night . . . and during your entire life. But the alcohol is no longer in your stomach, Juan Manuel, it's in your blood. And it's oozing from your left side. It hurts even to think about throwing up. Any movement of your body hurts, all the way to the middle of your chest. No, you don't want to throw up, just control the nausea with slow, easy breathing. That's it. In. Out. In. Out. In. Out. It's not exactly hunger that you feel, just chills in your stomach. You need some chicken soup from Caldos Zenón on San Juan de Letrán. They had really been changing the name from San Juan de Letrán to Eje Central. How ridiculous!

A bowl of chicken soup, or anything to warm up your stomach. In. Out. Your eyes are swollen and bloodshot. You would like to rub them, but you can't move your left hand; and if you move your right hand, it hurts your chest. Your irritated eyes and your back pockmarked with debris hurt more than the spot where there's a .38-caliber bullet lodged in your side. You close your eyes to allow your eyelids to lubricate your eyeballs. It doesn't help. They're too dry, dusty, and dirty. You've already cried all the tears you ever had in your life. You'll never cry again, Juan Manuel. You had just so many tears in your lifetime, and now you've used them up. You're dying, you bastard. Don't laugh. You're dying. You can't believe it. Your time has arrived. You're dying here, in the middle of the Zócalo, during this night that refuses to become day. And you're not going to see the light of day either. You're going to be dead when the street sweepers arrive to sweep you up, Barrientos, along with the rest of the garbage. You're going to be dead when, at the break of day, the soldiers play reveille and take your body to jail for having profaned the flagpole. You'll never have the chance to cure this hangover that you've been cultivating throughout the entire day. It will remain with you for all eternity. That is hell, Juan Manuel: an incurable, indolent, and endless hangover. You laugh because you can't believe this is happening. You can't believe that you're dying, just like that, uselessly, unjustifiably, in the middle of the Zócalo. Nevertheless, there you have it. You even sobered up out of fright. So you're done for, my dear Juan Manuel. Are you aware of that? There's a bullet in your side. You're bleeding. Little by little, the sticky pool next to you gets bigger and bigger. It's all the way up your back, or at least that's what you feel. Off to your right, you hear moaning. It was always there, but you hadn't paid any attention to it. You thought it was you, your own breathing, now so difficult, that was bouncing off the silence around you. But no, it's someone else's breathing. It must be one of the thieves. The one who went down first, flat on his face, right before your frightened eyes. You can still see the expression on his face when the bullet hit him—terror and resignation, simultaneously. He was young, very young, barely a kid. Like a wounded dog, the kid whimpers slightly as if he were licking his wounds. Opening your eyes wide, you look to your right and see a body facedown on the ground. His whimpering turns to a more audible stammering. He says something, but you can't understand what he's trying to say, or what he wants to say. You only hear him repeat some words that you're unable to decipher, as if he were speaking a foreign language, even though it contains the universal meaning of pain, fear, and perhaps repentance. Everything is rolled together—a guttural burp, indecipherable, from the heart just before it stops beating. You feel sorry for him. Unlike you, he probably wanted to live, you think. He was barely a kid, almost a child. You can see him, several feet away, arms and legs outstretched, facing you. You perk up your ears, trying to understand what he is repeating over and over again. It's useless. Even though you've already memorized his moaning and can repeat it exactly like him, it still doesn't make sense. No matter. Even though you can't translate it, somehow you're able to understand him. And somehow you manage to respond, not with words, but with a corresponding whimper that calms him down and stops his moaning. Finally, silence. Sadly, you hold your breath for a few seconds as you strain to hear a breath, but you hear nothing more, only the silence of the eternal night. He's screwed, you conclude. You cast a glance at the cadaver and, despite the darkness, think you see your wine-colored Italian loafers on his feet. Trying to run in loafers? That's dumb! I should have put on my tennis shoes this morning, you think. If I had done that, maybe this bastard wouldn't be lying here dead. You close your eyes, but you're afraid that your parched eyelids will stick together and you'll never be able to open them again. You open them again. You turn your head in the other direction—to the left. You see the other body, now inert. He is wearing your tweed sport coat, perforated in the back, at about the level of his kidneys. You spot the knife next to him on the ground, the one that he put to your throat. Who would ever have thought you were going to serve as a shield, Juan Manuel? It was always other people who shielded you, yes, other people . . . and alcohol.

He was stupid to use you as a shield. He's dead. You can't even be a shield. How long has it been since you were shot? Who knows? It all happened so fast, amid so much confusion, and now time is standing still. You feel like you've lain here hours, bleeding away, but it's probably been only a matter of minutes, because you haven't heard the cathedral bell ring once since you've been there! Let it be daybreak, damn it! Why doesn't someone pass by here, see me, help me? Son of a bitch, I'm dying. You want to scream for help, but the pressure in your chest prevents you. Anyway, who would hear you? Your voice would be but a whisper in the middle of the Zócalo. It would like trying to light up the immense plaza with a match. Were there four or five? Six, yes, six shots were fired. He had emptied his gun. One bullet for each of you, the rest missed their mark. You don't remember very well what happened next, only that it sounded like machine-gun fire after they shot at you and these guys, a rapid fire burst like an eruption of flame. Then your pursuers were chased away, the ones who had fired at you and your thieves. Pursued pursuers. That's why they didn't come over and finish you off and these guys who died with you. And they would've finished you off. Maybe right now your assassins are flat on their backs, like you, slowly dying or now dead in the Zócalo. Maybe they managed to escape. Who knows? There's dead silence everywhere. No one is around. Time has stopped. Let it be daybreak, damn it! Why can't someone come by here? Doesn't anyone see that I'm going to hell in a hand basket? Please, let it be daybreak. Oh, Juan Manuel, even if it takes you a hundred years to die, daylight won't come until you're dead. The sky is totally dark. You still can't make out any shapes. There's no moon, no clouds, either, or at least you can't make them out from where you are. The shitty air blocks your vision of the sky. You look over at the cathedral. This afternoon, which now seems as far away as your childhood, you refused to look at it from the front. You chose to go around it, down Monte de Piedad, Guatemala, Seminario. You looked at from all sides and from the back, but you didn't see it, as you're doing now. Why did you settle for looking at the west steeple only, Juan Manuel? Your eyes minutely scanned every bit of it, so that you could explain to Fernando and Jimena the different styles that over the centuries had been superimposed on the structure. But neither Fernando nor Jimena is with you now, Juan Manuel. And, what's more, who gives a damn about those styles now, with those dumb columns, bases, and spires. If you're dying, who gives a damn about anything you've ever learned or taught? You didn't want to look at the cathedral straight on, because it was too big and imposing for you. It made you feel despicable, humiliated. To look straight at it signified an effort as brutal as what it took to build it. But now, you feel close to it, as if it were your home. Since you're nearsighted, you lift your gaze upward toward the twin steeples and the bell towers on top, the theological icons of virtue that crown the monumental clock hiding time from you, toward the ornamented balustrades around the nave, and visualize that light, invisible from your vantage point, coming from the gigantic lantern inside the central dome that off-sets the corpulence of the steeples. This is the last time you'll contemplate the cathedral, and you begin to imagine with some arrogance that as soon as you die—immediately following your asinine, stupid death—the cathedral will begin to fall apart, the steeples will break away, and everything will come tumbling down. You're dying like a common, stray dog. Alone. No one's around. You're alone, smack in the middle of the most populous city on the planet. Where are your children? What children? I don't have any children. Where is your wife? What wife? I don't have a wife. Where are your friends, Juan Manuel? They vanished during all those drunken sprees. Why did you let them take your children from you? Why don't you ever look for them? You could have seen them, even if from hiding. Or you could have written to them. Pure selfishness. Vanity. I hope they feel my absence. But the one who feels the absence is you, especially now that you're going to hell in a hand basket. Even if they were to show up at this very moment, you wouldn't recognize them and they wouldn't recognize you. They would simply turn around and walk away. And they're not going to suffer because of your death as you suffered because of your father's death. How could they if they don't even know who you are. To them, you've been dead since you abandoned them. You substituted your students for your children. Generation after generation passed through the classroom of your words, but now even they're not here to take notes. Why have they abandoned you? Who gave you that kiss on the cheek? You can still detect that fetid smell and visualize that toothless mouth and greasy hair. You feel your sore cheekbone again. Who the hell was he? Where did he come from? And the dead man in your closet? Who was that kid? He had glassy eyes, like you. Who will inherit your suits, Juan Manuel? And your ties and shoes? Your books? Your notes? Your manuscripts? Who in hell gives a damn, anyway? How you wish that Jimena were here right now, holding your left hand. With a caress, perhaps she could revive you. You wish she would appear in front of you right now, like that first time she appeared in your office. And you wish Fernando would show up, if only to dig out that damn bullet that's perforated your kidneys. And Antonio . . . oh, Antonio. You have saved me from so many altercations. And, now, you could help me remove that flask that's pressing against my right buttock. You're thirsty. You taste the thick saliva that you can't swallow or spit out. You need a drink. Lodged between your body and the ground, your flask will be hard to reach, because you can't move. And your Sancho Panza—Antonio—isn't there with you. But, frankly, thirst might just overcome immobility and pain. You draw your right hand closer to your body. You run it along the ground until you touch your leg. Then you bend your elbow until your hand reaches your butt. Now comes the hard part, because you have to use your abdominal muscles in order to be able to stick your hand under your body. Knowing that it's going to hurt, you think about it a second or two. You don't have any strength left. Only your thirst can overcome this centuries-long fatigue that makes you dizzy. You make an unsuccessful attempt. You can't do it. You take a breath. In. Out. In. Out. In. Out. You wait a seemingly long time before making another attempt. Your chest hurts, but your right hand reaches the pocket with that flask, which contains your last sip, the last sip of your life. Now you have to pull it out. You can feel the top of the flask and its silver cap, but you have to raise your stomach in order to pull it out of your pocket. You take a breath and make a laborious attempt to raise your rear end from the pavement. It hurts everywhere and you scream. The scream itself hurts, but you finally manage to pull it out. There it is, in your right hand. You rest for a minute. You breathe. In. Out. In. Out. In. Out. You let a long while pass and concentrate on unscrewing the cap with only your right hand. It isn't easy, because you don't have enough agility in your fingers. You slowly caress the threads of the cap, trying to make it easier to unscrew, but it's too difficult. After a long struggle, you manage to get the cap off, but it falls to the ground and rolls away. You aren't able to sit up in order to take a sip. No matter, because the flask is almost empty, and its meager contents aren't going to spill out. Putting it on your chest, you swiftly insert the opening of the flask into your mouth. You swallow the last drink of your life, Juan Manuel, right down to the last drop. But it tastes like vinegar. For a moment, it dissolves the thick saliva stuck to your tongue, and you imagine that the alcohol is disinfecting your wounds. Okay, I promise . . . for sure this time I'll never drink again. And you laugh at yourself. You laugh at yourself for the last time. Come closer, Alejandra, and let me inhale your perfume. You look so pretty with that dyed dark lock of hair. Let me enjoy the fragrance of your neck and caress you with this hand, because I can't with the other one. It's dead. You once told me that you'd never reach fifty years of age. Do you remember, Alejandra? I'm never going to be fifty years old. And you never were. Your beauty and youth made you overly confident, and you had said it out of vanity, only two weeks after a birthday. Nevertheless, death took charge of confirming what you had predicted. You never reached fifty years of age, Alejandra. At the time, Alejandra, I was a little younger than you, but if it makes you feel any better, now I'm older than you. Now you can be fifty years old. We'll celebrate your birthday together. I'll invite you to eat lobster at El Danubio, and later that evening we'll have a few martinis at

Las Sirenas, or in the Oak Bar in New York, whatever you would prefer. A few martinis made with Bombay Sapphire, a tiny drop of bitters, and no vermouth. And we'll make love fifty times in order to celebrate each year of your life. Fernando! Fernando, please take that piece of metal out of my back. You can't imagine how much it hurts. Have you seen my keys, Jimena? How can I leave without my keys? I don't have any keys or glasses. Not even my pens. I can't leave without glasses, Jimena, my sweetheart. This ship is rolling too much. I'm seasick. When will we reach land? Fernando, here's Jimena. Take good care of her. Love her. Make her happy. I give you my mother, too. Take care of her. Mom, when you died you took your hands with you; without your caresses, you've left my head mutilated. Mom, buy me something at Dulcería Celaya, so I can die in peace. Damn it, this ship is really rolling back and forth now. I'm feeling seasick. I want to vomit. When will we reach land? Can you hear me, Dad? If not, listen to me. Get me off this ship. Take me to land. Don't abandon me.

· · · · ·

A few, tiny insignificant pebbles began to bounce off the stone bell that sat atop the western steeple of the cathedral. Some were stopped in their downward plunge by the stone wreath that surrounded such an unusual crown, while others continued to fall with the almost imperceptible sound of sand in an hourglass until they reached the priests' balcony. After a short while, a cracking sound crossed the path of the falling pebbles and created a fissure that began at the pinnacle sustaining the weight of a sphere that, in turn, served as the base of the topmost cross of the steeple and ended at the opening of the monumental bell. At first, sand and pebbles continued to fall through the new crack, but now accompanied by larger stones and rocks. Soon, the growing fissure freed the pivot that held the sphere and pediment together, and the sphere, whose proportions could not be appreciated from below, began its precipitous fall. Before anyone could say amen, the crucifix sustained by the sphere hit one of the saints that flanked the balustrade of the upper balcony. In one fell swoop, it decapitated him and thus ratified, as with any martyr, his sanctity. Not unlike a high-speed cannon ball, it spiraled downward, completely destroying the neoclassic balustrade designed by Tolsá before hitting the atrium with some Paleolithic sound of rock against rock as it took out a good part of the iron grating that incarcerated the cathedral. A pregnant silence announcing calamity ensued, which was followed by an expanding, deafening roar. It didn't come from outside but from inside the cathedral, escaping through the cracks in the doors, the belfries, and the stained-glass windows, which were breaking apart. The gigantic lantern in the dome looked like a factory chimney, out of which poured, like dense smoke, the clamor of catastrophe that was maturing like a thick, bubbly gush in the bowels of the cathedral. From the street, you could hear the shaking altarpieces, the grunting organs, the rainstorm of broken glass against the pews, floors, and altars. It was easy to visualize what was happening inside the church: angels were flying around the naves like bats; saints—crippled and intimidated after so many centuries of contemplation and lack of exercise—were trying to escape by putting into practice their rusty levitation talent; and the ten thousand virgins that formed part of the altarpieces darted with terror from chapel to chapel. The rumbling seemed to come from deep inside the earth, from the devastated pyramids below the surface, from the thin layers of the earth's substrata. The cathedral couldn't contain the rumbling, which was unable to vent itself through the bell towers or open windows. The initial fissure that had split the dome of the stone bell began to multiply like lightning throughout the steeples, the façade, and the adornments. All of a sudden, one of the torch holders that crowned the central clock fell to the ground, extinguishing it forever. The balustrades began to fall like so many teeth pulled from their stone gums. Agitated by fear and with a clamor felt throughout the center of the city, the bells seemed to leap headlong into space on their own accord. Due to their attributes and having lived in luxury in their niches in the façades of the cathedral and Metropolitan Chapel, the saints abandoned their places. The angels were unable to stop them from plummeting to earth on their own accord and breaking into pieces upon impact, conquered by Lucifer, who had waited millennia to avenge the timeless era of Genesis. Faith, Hope, and Charity, accompanied by their respective icons—the Cross, the Child, the Chalice—plummeted downward, terrified, piloting the clock, which smashed into pieces in the atrium. For a while, the rumbling seemed to attenuate, but only to catch its breath. Moments later, after a short respite, it returned with cataclysmic force in the center of the cathedral. Soon after, the erect lantern, so proud of its prodigious height, copulated with the dome and drove itself vertically straight into it, only to plunge into the cross vault below, now sucked into, swallowed up, and devoured by the edifice itself. That was the beginning of the end. With the loss of the lantern—flagpole, mast, antenna, lance, phallic symbol—the cathedral lost the marker of its columns, many of which lost their bases and now were swinging like wayward pendulums. Similarly, now tired of holding up the walls for centuries, the buttresses, like rebels, begin to push against them. As if the air in its upper body were escaping all at once, and given the volatility of its bell towers and the fragility of its articulations, the steeple to the west—ungraceful and breathless—began to implode. After another tremor that announced its fate, it fell noisily onto itself, accompanied by the excessive clamor of its fifty-two bells. The steeple on the east side followed in the steps of its twin and broke off into the sanctuary. Now exposed by the falling steeples that had contained it, and exhausted by the weight of the clock, the principal façade of the front of the church folded in the middle as if to go down on its knees, so that the bottom part fell forward and the top part fell backward in a sound like an earthquake. After the upheaval, there was peace and quiet. Even though the Zócalo was still completely shrouded with a dense cloud of dust, the convulsive trembling ceased. Silence followed, except for the occasional sound of rocks and debris settling into the enormous mound that was once the cathedral—spires, columns, cornices, mutilated saints and angels, bells, wedge-shaped stones from arches, corbels and brackets, bas-reliefs, crosses, twisted steel, displaced balustrades, empty niches, molding, torch holders, the pontifical coat of arms, and due to the simple law of gravity, the clock, now sitting on top of the remains of the façade that had sustained it, with its hands indicating 6:30, either morning or afternoon.

CHAPTER 13

I T WAS MORE night than day when they opened the main doors of the National Palace. A light but intense mist was falling on the plaza.

The city's street cleaners had already used their oversized brooms to sweep the immensity of the Zócalo and to create four enormous piles of garbage, one at each corner, like four small chapels belonging to the timeless cathedral.

Carrying the national flag, a military squad exited the palace.

Played out of tune, reveille announced a new day. The bugler signaled the beginning of the ritual, and the military band accompanied the ceremony with its drums. The flag—flaccid, musty, and still immersed in dreams—was raised on the flagstaff and received the honors that are customarily accorded that national symbol.

Justo Gómez, a soldier, who was standing the closest to the flagstaff, didn't realize that he was standing in a pool of blood that the wet mist hadn't managed to dissolve. A shiny object on the ground, stuck to the base, distracted him from his customary salute. Since he had been the first soldier to leave the palace, he would be the last one to go back inside. The bugler sounded the about-face and a return at double time. When everyone had advanced, the soldier Justo Gómez kicked the shiny object to put it in reach of his step, and without his superiors noticing, he picked it up as he passed and stuck it into the back pocket of his olive green uniform. Minus a lid, it was an empty silver hip flask that had the initials J.M.B.A. engraved on it, the only I.D. that Juan Manuel Barrientos Ahumada would have had to identify himself when they transported him to the Green Cross with two other cadavers, one identified as wearing a tweed coat and the other sporting a pair of wine-colored loafers.

CHAPTER 14

IT WASN'T RAINING hard, just a light drizzle, or an annoying heavy mist. However, if it didn't stop, it might ruin their Saturday.

Antonio walked into Salón La Luz at 12:09 p.m. He thought Dr. Barrientos would be waiting for him, because his punctuality was legendary. They were supposed to meet exactly at noon, yet the professor hadn't arrived. What a relief, he thought. He didn't want to be scolded in that subtle way that he was when he arrived late to class. You are the graduate assistant, don't do that to me. That "me" was some sort of possessive and offensive reprimand that always upset Antonio. Given the nature of the academic and personal relationship that had developed over the years, it was insignificant. Antonio was the most senior student of the professor's seminar. As his graduate assistant, while he had to perform some unpleasant duties for the professor, such as prepare bibliographies for the classes and correct his classmates' papers, he did have certain privileges, one being the possibility of launching his academic career alongside one the most prestigious, albeit controversial, professors on campus. True, he didn't have an easy relationship with the professor, especially the part of the relationship outside the university environment. Juan Manuel was an excessively demanding friend; yet, curiously enough, that's what made him so magnetic. His students were his life, and he was always disposed to showing the depth of his friendship. However, he always demanded the same in return. And, somehow, he always got it. Although their fascination for him bordered on fear, almost slavery—and especially when he drank, he created irritation and contempt in them—they still admired and loved him.

Javier and Amelia had already arrived at Salón La Luz. They were new students and had never accompanied their professor on one of his "city tours," as Juan Manuel called those incursions into the center of the city, in opposition to calling it "fieldwork," which biologists, geographers, geologists, and even economists. Antonio sat down with them.

"Juan Manuel isn't here yet, right?" he asked, accentuating the professor's first name in order to distinguish from the title, *Doctor*, which the new students used when referring to him.

"No, we haven't seen him, and we got here before noon. They hadn't even opened up yet. It must be the rain."

In a matter of minutes, the others arrived—Patricia, Catalina, with youthful joy; Pancho, Héctor, Julia—all of whom were excited about going on an excursion through the center of their own city about which they knew so little.

They pulled two tables together on which they quickly dropped their backpacks and notebooks, making the event look like a real field trip and not just an anthropological tour of downtown bars.

"Where's the professor?" Julia asked.

"Who knows?" said Antonio. "Strange that he's not here already."

"He's always so punctual."

It was raining outside. They ordered coffee. It's too early for a beer.

"But this is a bar, not a coffee shop."

While they waited for the others to arrive, Héctor and Antonio decided to order beers.

"Who's missing?"

"Fernando and Jimena."

"And Susana."

They brought out the beers first, which were warmish. Then came the coffees, which were also lukewarm.

After Susana entered the establishment, the swinging doors kept flapping back and forth. She ordered a beer before greeting anyone.

Now only Jimena and Fernando were missing.

When he was leaving Juan Manuel's house on Thursday night or, more precisely, in the wee hours of Friday morning, Fernando had taken Jimena home and suggested they go on the excursion together on Saturday. He had hoped that at some point he and Jimena could ditch the group and go off by themselves, have dinner together, perhaps at Bar León, listen to some music, go dancing, and . . . and so he drove his red Chevy to pick up Jimena at 11:00 a.m. Since she wasn't quite ready to go when he arrived, they got a late start. They parked the car in a lot on Venustiano Carranza, in front of a tall, narrow Porfirian mansion that had been transformed into a vertical restaurant with a horizontal name, El Malecón—The Breakwater—that was just around the corner from Salón La Luz. Given that the professor, without whom the excursion wouldn't take place, hadn't arrived yet, getting there late wasn't such a big deal.

Jimena and Fernando sat down with the group. In order to kill time with the others, Fernando ordered a beer. In an act of solidarity, Jimena did the same. Juan Manuel would have been shocked to see Jimena drink straight from the bottle, but that's what she did.

By then, it was 12:30 p.m. and Dr. Barrientos still hadn't arrived.

"Wasn't the plan to meet here?"

"Of course."

"And at noon?"

"At noon on the dot on Saturday. Salón la Luz."

"Do you think he forgot?"

"No way, man. He doesn't forget these things. It's like a class for him. He's never missed one. And he's never been late either."

"How strange. Maybe something happened to him?"

"Antonio, why don't you give him a call? Here's my cell phone."

Antonio punched in Juan Manuel's number, and he could visualize the phone ringing in the professor's house. No answer. He remembered that Juan Manuel had stayed home after the party. He was quite drunk, that's for sure, but he did confirm the meeting for the following day. Antonio heard from outside the professor locking his door. He also knew that the professor had gone by his office that morning. He had called him at midday, and the secretary said that Dr. Barrientos had been there earlier, but that he had an appointment off campus and would not return until Monday.

"No answer. If it's okay with you guys, let's wait a little bit longer."

Héctor and Antonio ordered more beers. Susana followed suit. Fernando and Jimena continued to sip their first one. The others ordered more coffee . . . but this wasn't a coffee shop.

By the time 1:00 p.m. had rolled around, the professor still hadn't arrived. Without him, there would be no excursion. And there was no teaching assistant who could lead the group either. Disillusioned, Amelia and Javier, who had been the first ones to arrive, decided to leave. Maybe another time. Julia and Pancho left with them. Patricia and Catalina said they were going for a walk, but they didn't go, at least while the others were still there. Seated in a booth toward the back, given that the mist was putting a damper on their hopes, were the ones who from the beginning had ordered beer, not coffee. Antonio and Héctor, Susana, Fernando, and Jimena.

Héctor hadn't eaten breakfast and ordered a sandwich of uncooked meat, which Susana then felt like having as well. They shared it and ordered another, which they also shared.

"What now? asked Susana.

"I don't know," said Antonio. "I've been with him many times on these walking tours, and each time they're different, but I do know which places he frequents the most."

It was a pity that Juan Manuel was not with them, yet why should they cancel everything, given that they were already downtown?

"Why don't we look for him in the places he likes the best? And we can have a drink in each one of them?" proposed Héctor.

Not a bad idea. They were already in the downtown area, and they were all ready to walk from bar to bar.

"Maybe we'll even find him."

"It's a shame if we don't, but it doesn't make sense to stay here. It's already 1:30."

"Nevertheless, let's keep trying to call him along the way."

Antonio paid the bill.

"I'll pick up the next one," said Héctor.

"So, where do we begin?"

"Let's go to La Ópera," said Antonio, having inherited the baton of the orchestra conductor.

Walking against the rain, or amid a heavy mist, they went to La Ópera, ate in the Bar Alfonso, stopped at Dulcería Celaya, went to La Puerta del Sol, contemplated the western steeple of the cathedral, went up to the terrace of La Casa de las Sirenas (where they didn't recognize a familiar umbrella waiting for its owner at the bar), wandered around Seminario Plaza, went into El Nivel, and then called it quits. The professor wasn't anywhere. They could have continued down Moneda, but they were afraid to walk down those streets when the streetlights were beginning to replace the remains of the day. Even though they had drunk in moderation, they were exhausted and slightly tipsy. Except for Héctor, the others didn't even drink in some bars. He had purchased a drink in each bar, and now he was ready to continue with Susana into the night. Let's go to Bar Mata, he urged, and Bar-roco, Bolívar 12, El Emporio, and Garibaldi, but his suggestions were not heeded by anyone. Arriving at the Zócalo, they all said good-bye to each other. Antonio and Susana took Héctor with them. Jimena and Fernando were finally alone, in the plaza, excited.

Once the rain had abated in the late afternoon, the shell dancers reinitiated the rhythms of their drums, bystanders congregated in hoards, and the national flag waved patriotically from the flagstaff in the middle of the plaza. Night was coming on.

In order to view the Zócalo in its entirety, Fernando suggested they go to the bar at the top of the Hotel Majestic. Jimena agreed enthusiastically.

They walked into the deep orange-colored reception area of the hotel and pressed the button of the ancient elevator. The doors opened, then the folding gate. The elevator operator took them to the top floor. The mist had driven off the tourists, so now the terrace was empty, all theirs. A few raindrops trickled off the umbrellas, but the tables and chairs were almost totally dry. A friendly waiter seated them at the table closest to the cathedral, but not before wiping off the glass tabletop and the plastic chair cushions. Fascinated by the urban landscape laid out before their eyes, they sat down. The flag and the National Palace were directly in front of them. The dome of Santa Teresa la Antigua was off in the distance. Washed and shiny from the rain, the cathedral was to the left, practically at arm's reach.

"It looks brand new," said Fernando.

"As if they had built it this morning," added Jimena.

"In just one day?" asked Fernando, laughing.

"Yes, in just one day," she responded.

• • • • •

In just one day, Jimena and Fernando built their own cathedral. They discovered that they liked the same movies, the same books, the same music. Similarities and differences. The same fears, the same desires. At the Majestic Hotel that night, they realized that they agreed on many things, all of which led to jesting, humor, love, and, simultaneously, the same laughter. A slight touch of the fingers. A caress. The brushing of the knees. Feigned anger. The exchange of breaths. Secret codes. Caresses on the neck. Sighing together. The first moist kiss with new lips. The eloquent silence. The everlasting gaze into each other's eyes.

"Wait here a moment," said Fernando. He went down to the reception desk, filled out a registration card, invented a story about nonexistent luggage, used his credit card for the first time, and went back to the terrace carrying the key to room 607 in his pocket. On the top floor, looking out onto the Zócalo, please.

And he commanded that the National Palace remain where it was, that the amber lights illuminating the cathedral remain lit until 11:00 p.m., which is when they turn them off, that the dome of Santa Teresa la Antigua remain standing, that the national flag continue waving on the flagstaff. He ordered a bottle of white wine, chilled, and he toasted Jimena, with Jimena, the two of them, and their eternal love.

Before the cathedral lights went dark, they went down to the floor below. Fernando opened the door to room 607. Jimena acted surprised. While Fernando turned on the lamp on the night table, Jimena went out onto the balcony. Fernando followed her, and they both saw the same thing that they had seen from the terrace above. As Fernando had commanded, the National Palace was still there, the cathedral lights were still on, the dome of Santa Teresa la Antigua hadn't fallen, and the flag waved gently in the breeze. They kissed on the balcony, in the center of downtown, the very heart of the city, in front of the Zócalo. They kissed, laughed, nibbled on each other, hugged, and kissed again. Back in the hotel room, they undressed slowly, getting to know each other, recognizing each other, because they already had an image of each other. They had hopes. They desired each other. Surprisingly, they enjoyed each other's playfulness. And they made love. More than once. Naked and confused, they fell asleep together.

· · · · ·

The sound of reveille in the plaza woke Fernando. Still naked, he jumped out of bed and went to the door of the balcony, partially covering himself with the curtains. He had never known at what time the military squad raised the national flag every morning, which they were preparing to do now, accompanied by the roll of the drums of war in the immensity of the plaza. Jimena slept peacefully, with a finger in her mouth. Fernando heard all the orders played by the bugler, and when the last soldier was inside the National Palace, he got back into bed and embraced Jimena, who wasn't even aware of the flag ceremony. He went back to sleep.

They woke up just after 10:00 a.m. They caressed each other, kissed with now sore lips, got up, showered together, washed each other, splashed water on each other as if they were little kids in a swimming pool, and put on their same clothes. Hand in hand, they went up to the terrace to have breakfast. They didn't let go of each other until they had to serve themselves from the buffet. They were hungry and thirsty. They sat down at the same table as the night before. With a feeling of fulfillment hardly tarnished by the pain of having to say good-bye soon, they minimized the dimensions of the immense Zócalo.

Downstairs, while Jimena observed a collection of ceramics adorning the reception area, Fernando paid the bill as if it were an everyday occurrence.

They decided to walk to the parking lot where the Chevy had spent the night. Hand in hand, they walked down Cinco de Mayo and looked at the same storefronts, buildings, doors, and cobblestones. When they got to Filomeno Mata, they turned left and went down Gant toward Venustiano Carranza.

In Salón La Luz, the impeccable Dr. Juan Manuel Barrientos—tweed sport coat, dark shirt, colorful tie—was drinking a beer at one of the sidewalk tables, behind the plants that delineated the space. It was straight up noon, and the sun overhead illuminated the gray hairs on his temples and gave a certain luminescence to his gaze toward the street down which Fernando and Jimena were walking. The infatuated couple passed right by him. The metal shutters were closed, the table umbrellas were folded shut, and there were no rustic chairs behind the large potted plants.

Salón La Luz doesn't open on Sundays.